Henry
A Novel of Beer and Love in the West

Michael Strelow

DEDICATION

This book is dedicated to the western story tellers of all times and places. Stories show us how we can live.

CONTENTS

ACKNOWLEDGMENTS

I want to express thanks to the Oregon Historical Society and its archives and staff, the Oregon State Library, and the numerous small museums and archives across Oregon where I pursued the material for this novel. The single most valuable source was the book by E. Kimbark MacColl, *The Shaping of a City: Business and Politics in Portland, Oregon 1885 to 1915*. Important thanks go to my wife, Lynne, for her patience, dedication, persistence, proofreading and her care and feeding of the author.

Whatever is done from love always occurs beyond good and evil.

Friedrich Nietzsche

Chapter One

In the Winter Garden

I am sitting in the winter garden, what is now being called the herbarium or the greenhouse, but what I have known as a winter garden all my life. I am sitting thinking about love and the strength of love and how love is like these tropical plants growing in here while outside is this Portland, Oregon winter raining down cold rain day after day. How impossible and fragile is love. I have a blanket over my knees, this wicker chair, and I have also recently these thoughts, again, about love.

When I think of history—even my own history—I exclude myself from it in order to look at it. I find it over there, apart from me and the blanket across my knees, and I have to summon it like calling a dog. It comes eventually, wagging its tail.

I would like to listen to the wicker creak and think of the love story only and lump together all the rest in one other heap, but they come together—Mrs. Els, someone else's wife—the brewery with the song of barrels being coopered together, the Oompah band, the deer carcasses hanging just outside the fire, the backs of the teamster's horses steaming in the rain…

When I came to America I was not looking for love—but I found it. I was not looking for death, but I found it. I was young and what did I know of death? I was full of German stories about Indians and gold and impossible scenes under western stars. I thought I would be chased by bears, and then I would brew the world's finest beer and everyone would beat a path to my door. There would be bags of money marked clearly with dollar signs. I didn't know there would also be Beethoven and orchards of pink and white as far as I could see. And out of it all would come the love story, my love story and the siren song, temptation of biblical proportions—lots of biblical proportions in the American West.

I tuck the blanket tighter—my bad knee, the chill in my kidneys, my left shoulder—and my story warms me. I don't worry about my agenda in telling the story, my agenda in which I am more than just lucky somehow, maybe chosen, maybe just German and the son of my father's exceedingly tidy workbench. I am all of those and?…and that other thing love does to every story, a tincture that stains every event and surprise and drop of blood on velvet. I won't even pretend to be telling this with any impartiality. How could I? I loved and that was, for the time anyway, that was everything.

Chapter Two

Portland, Oregon

The water is awful, and it makes men so sick they can't work. And if they can't work, no one makes any money. Better they drink beer. It keeps them healthy and healthy men are good workers. Everybody makes a living.
The woods come right to the edge of town like the *Schwarzwald* in the old country—dark, and heavy with moisture and dead branches. The only difference is that here the woods don't have any stories. In Germany there were tales of woodsmen and their families, of witches and evil spirits and things that lived in live oak branches and lived in dead oak branches. The stories were of familiars and monsters that filled the woods, and you only had to spend a night there to get in touch with both. These Oregon woods, on the other hand, are waiting for their stories although some tell me that the Indians have their share already; they are always reluctant tell us what they are.

So we'll fill the woods eventually, I suppose. But right now it's just sweat and cursing. The men are glad for the wages, come into town each night thirsty and can't drink the foul water without the risk of losing three days' wages

3

bent over shooting yellow water out the top end and black
out the bottom. The Indians laugh at them and have a
word they tell me means something like "bad camper."
The beer is a good answer to the whole situation. The men
come in thirsty, they drink my beer until they're not thirsty
anymore, and then they look up from the beer and want
women. Lately, I've been able to supply them with both.

It started when one bar run by a drunken Englishman,
Bartholomew Cummings, who had no self-discipline and
who couldn't keep his employees from stealing from him,
couldn't pay his beer bill two months in a row. He was
relieved to find I would take a percentage of his business
and forgive the bill. Within six months I had a quarter of
his business, within a year, half. I put in the girls upstairs
then, and that boosted both of our takes. He proved to be
quick learner at first and saw the possibilities of the added
revenue. The girls were tractable, easier to work with than
the men in the bar. But he kept up his drinking and bad
management. And then he couldn't keep his hands off the
girls. And that was the end of that. I owned most of his
bar by then, so I fired him. He hung around cursing me to
the workers, drunk and sober. Maligning me to my own
workers in front of my own brewery. Most of my workers
didn't speak much English so it didn't really matter, but
still, the principle of the thing was at stake. His antics
drunk and sober continually aggrieved me, though no one
in the Portland German community gave him any credence.
He began to allege among strangers that I had stolen his
business and was running a house of vice against

community standards, that I paid off police. My reputation as a sound businessman held its ground for all who knew of me. But so many strangers were coming into Portland in 1868, and Cummings was spending all his waking hours on his defamation project, that finally I knew I had to do something.

I had two new workers, Thomas and Johann, young men straight from my home region of Wurttemberg in Germany. Neither spoke English or had any friends outside the German community in town. I explained to them what this Englisher was about each day, his unrelenting project to shame me in my new hometown. How I had even offered him a modest stake to leave town and go try his luck elsewhere in the West. How he spit at my offer. Shook his fist at me. Called me the vile names that his English language is so efficient at. They both understood my chagrin, of course. And almost at the same time, they asked me what they could do to help. The one was an apprentice cooper, Johann, with forearms like the oak he worked, like the iron hoops he hammered into place. The other, Thomas, also a cooper, rolled barrels all day up the ramps and into the wagons. Both strong young men. I said I thought that Cummings might forget his bile if he were convinced that I truly felt he should no longer pursue his public vilification. They nodded and looked at each other.

I heard later that Cummings was taken to the edge of town hog-tied in a wagon and there the two young men decided that the way they could convince him of their

seriousness, of my displeasure, was to beat him severely. I
never saw the results of the beating, but I heard that
Cummings was missing most of his front teeth, had one
eye drooping and sightless, and walked with a marked limp
before he was well enough to leave town. I have to say that
I would not have prescribed such harsh medicine for so
small a malady as Cummings. But the young men being
young men decided on their own both the medicine and
the dosage. I recognized quickly that their punishment was
in keeping with the Old World version of civility. That a
breach of etiquette against a man of my stature in the
community called for stern measures and that the whole
fabric of propriety itself was implicated in the effectiveness
of the message they conveyed to Cummings. I raised both
their wages as soon as possible but not so high as to
fracture the wage structure all workers expect. I watched
them both for signs of the high seriousness that precedes
promotion to more responsible positions.

The girls upstairs at the bar were rarely a problem.
There were squabbles, of course. But a strong leader
among the girls often stopped problems before they
manifested themselves. At first the managers tried to make
one of the white girls the leader who settled matters of
dissention. The Negroes and Italians would listen to her,
defer to her, he figured. But it quickly became obvious that
the girls would sort out their own leader based on
something besides skin color. It was never clear just what.
But the managers reported they let the girls do their own
politics, and that worked unless there were two very strong

girls at the same time with neither willing to take second place to the other. It turned out that stalemate was very rare for some reasons that were not entirely clear to any of us males.

After two years I had three bars with busy upstairs just like the first. What seemed like the accident of not paying the beer bill just continued to happen with the second and third. I didn't want any more bars or I could have had more. Germans owned almost half the bars in Portland. The improvident English and Irish just didn't seem to have the knack for running bars in the West, while Germans usually made a go of it—girls or no girls. But the girls provided a steady income, almost monotonous in its certainty. Through rainy, dark winter, sap rising in the spring, exhausting heat of late summer, the men treated themselves with perfect predictability to delights of the flesh.

The world of Portland was divided into two distinct camps—the family men and their families and then the men alone who worked the river and woods. And it was the men alone who drank more beer and used the girls to compensate for the lack of family and hearth. It was a poor alternative, but it seemed that the one might substitute perfectly for the absence of the other. At least it became clear that it was an economic certainty in a world of uncertain finances. Banks might fail from bad management, unlucky investments or the vicissitudes of international funding, but the girls gave good value and steady income.

The damn Scottish kept to themselves and hoarded their money and waited for certainties in a place of uncertainties. The men of Dundee, the Earl of Airlie, the Scots' Mercantile Guild—they hem and haw and feel their pockets as if they were missing the crooked farthing given them by a grandfather. They drink to excess only at home. They turn their heads away from an honest German money question as if I had asked them intimate details of their marriage beds. Reid the other day, fatuous greasy skinflint that he is, proposed a mercantile plan for the waterfront that would have shoveled dollars into his pockets out of the public coffers. Not that any of us wouldn't have loved the deal ourselves, but Reid had the bad taste to make the theft so obvious that it would have stood as an insult to every other businessman's acuity.

The young English males, on the other hand, seem to have a patent world view--they came into the Portland country well dressed, broke and waving around manners and then looking to see if they could find one of Captain Couch's daughters to marry. It happened enough times that it became a local joke. But the other English have been here from the beginning, the shrewd hard workers. Corbett, Failing, Couch and their henchmen are not as tight as the Scots but every one of them has some kind of sweetheart deal with an eastern supplier. You never see the tip of their money much less the base. Corbett ran deals around the San Francisco wholesalers for the first time years ago and never looked back. He and Failing now are so tight you couldn't slip a skinny Scot between them. They sit at meetings looking off into space as if they had no need to talk it over; they share a brain, some say.

But down at the river docks is where the machine that drives all of this commences its chugging. The day workers, whoever was the last to arrive with the least skills, walk the planks from the boats and wheel the warehouses full. Wheat for Spaulding's mill upstream, bolts of cloth headed for Corbett's storage, china and soap and wax and salt beef and plowshares and the tinker's solder—they all came in by boat until the railroad. The same men invested in the railroad who had the steamboat monopoly because they saw the changeover coming. It wasn't hard to see the handwriting on the wall, really. And the two—water and land—together just about tied up all the loose ends. Transport had to just sit back and watch the land fill up and create demand for their services. It's never that simple, of course. Some people need to die, some need to be cheated while the cheaters look over their shoulders waiting for the public anger. There needs to be veniality and civic conniving and self-serving. There needs to be great ideas, and beer has always been one of them.

Chapter Three

Beer is Magic

Beer stands for the transformation itself, from woods to stump field to house to mansion. Beer is magic. You start with some raw things and end up with a cooked thing far superior to any of the raw parts. The same relationship exists between a tree and a house, a boy and a man. There needs to be the transformation and it needs to be managed carefully or you end up building a falling down shack, making a criminal, concocting awful beer. It always surprises me how few men can do the managing of the magic.

On the way to Portland as a young man, I stopped in the Midwest to see if there was room for another brewer, another brewery. I found the Germans hunkered in place in every town big and small ready to fight anyone who would presume on their patent beer rights. Too many dogs, not enough bones. I worked for two years in Cincinnati to get money to continue my travels. Then I decided to try the West.

For a German young man coming into the West in 1856, there were endlessly fascinating sights, endlessly engaging tales. Back in Germany we knew stories of the

West, but each one seemed like the fairy tales old people told to scare children and make them behave. The old German story of the mother who threatened to cut the thumbs off her children if they didn't behave, that was my personal favorite—so German, so Grimm. But tales that leaked back to Europe from the American West now seem like odd and desperate concoctions. The Indians who protected the white stranger who, lost and hungry, came to live among them, then when they tired of the white guest, they simply killed him and let him lie for the animals to eat—this story seemed to have a life of its own in Germany as if the uncivil cruelty contained a lesson about the New World. I never heard it even once after I came to America; it was wholly a resident of Europe. And there were tales of inferior animals that were actually miniatures of the European version—deer or badgers or elk. Hardly a snack for a white man but weak enough for the Indians to catch. Again, this story had no currency whatsoever in America. One story that proved true was a description of the Yellowstone country: sulfur boiling up out of the ground, pits of steam and blue hot water that waited until you were close and then shot in your face, whole plateaus full of the devil's own vents of hell fire, air so poison you passed out and fell into boiling water and were cooked alive. I suppose it was so fantastic—the truth and the tale—that both had to qualify as lies. Most of the European tales, after I had spent years in America, seemed to me simple attempts to protect the Old World against any possibility that the New World had anything superior. After all, God himself had chosen a pantheon of superior men and women to be Kings and Queens and then installed them in strategic capitols of Europe to rule and connive with each other to produce heirs to the thrones. This basic courtesy of God to man existed nowhere in America. George Washington, it seemed, failed to capitalize on his good fortune and perspicacity.

I wore my germanity like a great coat coming through the United States looking for a place for my brewery. I went first to southern Ohio where I had heard there was a strong and thriving German community, not to set up my brewery, but to get a feel for the country of immigrants. I came through New York but had been warned that I would find it tawdry and evil. And so it was. There was nothing I had experienced in Europe to match the human tragedy of New York—the smell of desperate people who had arrived without the ability to imagine an immense and empty country beyond the city of their entrance. The scale of the United States, its vastness, was literally unimaginable to immigrants at first. A train trip to Chicago—Halfway, it was known as—introduced us to size, size we had no model for in Europe. To ride a train for days and days and still be in the same country! The smell of too many people too close together in New York, yes, but also the smell there of ignorance and superstition and elemental hunger. I had been warned that New York City was a useful place to find a train to somewhere else—this from Germans who had come to America and returned, a theme in my home town that replayed itself in many different ways. These reports usually observed that the standard American immigrant in New York was filthy, dressed in rags and prey to his own people in some way. The most recently arrived went to work for the earlier arrivals who cheated and lied to them until they could discover what was really going on. It was a form of ethnic group slavery—Chinese did it to Chinese, Poles to Poles, Germans to Germans, Irish to Irish. It was something about language, something about cunning—an initiation ritual. Most of the new Irish came from towns where they had spoken only Irish and their English skills were minimal. The English had a hard time doing this nefarious business to other English because they caught on so much quicker having the language already.

I was leaving Germany in the first place not to flee the unpleasantness of the emerging political situation, the constant enmities and internecine warfare among the Germans themselves (many others fled this situation with its incumbent fiscal irresponsibility), but I was fleeing the fact that I would spend a lifetime working for someone else's brewery in Germany. I apprenticed to the trade, became competent, then expert, faster than my contemporaries, and then I found myself much in demand but destined to spend the rest of my life as brew master to a boss who would always be reaping the rewards of my cleverness, thrift and industry. The Hanseatic League had established brewing rights in the 15th century, and although they expanded somewhat, by the middle of the 19th century the rights to brew beer were all taken. I found the prospect of this form of slavery intolerable. In America I would be the boss. There would be places without breweries that would not only welcome me but make me first citizen, a burgher I could never have been in Germany.

I had heard that the first western communities immediately upon settling the West looked down at their feet and found themselves literally standing in the mud or dust unshod, their shoes consumed by the crossing. They sent word that the second wave should contain shoemakers. They would tire of drinking water, even good water, the same way. They would send for men who could brew good beer just as soon as their feet were warm and dry. Sit a man by a fire after a day's work, and he'll need a beer. Gather men and women together—beer, *gemutlich*.

Cincinnati. My first western American city, and it was full of Germans. The brewery business was already *besetzt* as we say in German, but there was work, and quickly my bosses found out that I knew what I was doing, and I became an assistant brewer.

I worked alongside an old man, the cousin of the head brewer, who constantly cursed in German, and when he was truly vexed, he would break out the vilest words he knew in English, words he had picked out of the frail English he had learned in ten years in Cincinnati—puke and dandruff. Eventually he combined them into pukey-dandruff, a word reserved for the disastrous failure of a batch of beer, an astronomical and crashing catastrophe. When I first heard him use this new hybrid, I thought I had become privilege to a potent curse, and so I saved my debut use for a fitting situation.

An apprentice cooper, a square-headed young man who couldn't keep his fingers out of his nose, had a barrel he was ill-making explode on him shooting the top hoop into the air along with a shower of staves. The hoop landed like a freed cat and raced across the shop, somehow made it around a corner and into the brewing area like a frightened, iron beast. I looked up at the hoop now raging for brewers to maim, and out of me exploded, "pukey-dandruff! *Pass auf!*" Brewers are usually not the swiftest of humans, being rounded off by their own tastings, inflated with the wind of sausage and cheese that accompany beer. But these Cincinnati brewers there at Koehler brothers displayed remarkable speed and agility as if they had suddenly seen their ancestors' ghosts clanging down upon them. Pukey-dandruff indeed! They dove behind brewing kettles, under the scaffolding they used to climb the sides of the kettles, behind mash pots while the hoop found a brick wall, rung out like a bell and wheeled into circular silence.

The idiot cooper peered around the corner to see what he could see. Brewers began reappearing from the crevices that had given them shelter. The young apprentice brewer (another relative of the boss) took out after the cooper brandishing a hygrometer he planned, according to his own announced plans, to stick up the ass of the cooper and break it off in there so he would be shitting glass for the rest of his life. The incident takes on in my memory a much more literary caste than it probably had. I was a young man, I had announced to my new country my linguistic ability, and the monotony of one day in Cincinnati had been shattered.

I lived simply in a room I rented in a house that leaked those wet Ohio winters into the very sleeping sheets at night. The cold off the Ohio River insinuated itself into my young bones. I discovered briefly a vile "brandy" the French riverboat men concocted from rotten fruit, and then I discovered the white lightning distilled by the Scotch-Irish. I much preferred the civility of good white lightning to the former. But I soon realized that either and both though they drove the cold out of my bones were substitutes for my own ambitions and plans, and so I stopped the indulgence altogether in the name of my future, my industry.

When I arrived in Cincinnati I thought it was the West. I found the river immediately, the rough beasts that worked the docks, the fabulously attired Frenchmen in their colored plumage recently arrived from the Missouri River drainage with pelts and stories to trade for whiskey and cats. Yes, cats. The Indians, the Mandans and the Sioux and Pawnees, found an early delight in the first cats the French brought with them. They traded well and hard for the cats, cats becoming a kind of second currency after whiskey. I think they ate some of them, but also were highly amused by the cats that did not grow large like the wild cats they knew—cougars. Their dogs, according to one source, immediately went to chasing the cats and killing the ones they could get. The dogs were severely disciplined and repeat offenders eaten. I loved the stories. They were exactly what I expected from my daydreaming of America while a young man in Germany. I could only imagine the cats and dogs scene, the flamboyant French, but as an article of faith I knew that America would be full of wonders I couldn't even begin to imagine. In Cincinnati there were signs and talismans of my imagined West, and so I was satisfied for a while.

I took my pay working in the Gottfried Koehler Brewery and except for room and board at a nearby rooming house, I put it in a German bank. I hired out to the Koehler brothers, Gottfried and Henry, because they recognized my old world credentials—my thorough apprenticeship in Stuttgart, my Swabisch discipline—despite my young years. At work I was surrounded by German speakers, and in the street had I chosen to stay in the brewery neighborhood, I could have spoken nothing but German. I resolved early on to get out among the Americans and learn English better. I worked with men who day and night never passed an English word through their lips.

The riverfront in Cincinnati became my American West. I could sit off to the side in the Alston bar, and not incidentally bawdyhouse, where America was devising itself along the Ohio River. The banjo band kept raucous rhythm on a raised stage, and this passed for music to align the hard drinkers with the easy drinkers. That first summer the heat came off the street and in the front door like a mountain, and out the back door at the outhouses the river rose up a cool sewer smelling of the collective bowels of the new country. From my corner, my back to the wall in the darkest shadows cast by the kerosene lamps I listened for America, listened for what I would have to become to make a home in these shadows.

The banjo band sweated and hammered the evening; they seemed to have no particular tune in mind but to stroke against the strings and stretched hides that gave back a quick heartbeat against the noise of the men. A fistfight off to my right was sudden and seemed in rhythm with the band. The other men ignored it until the two rolled into their feet, and then they kicked both men out from under the table, boots against man-meat until the silent punches fell without sound against the din, one man on top of the other in no hurry finally hitting and hitting in perfect rhythm with the band. The younger man, about my age, had disappeared under the gray, broad back of the shorter, older man who finally slowed, arm weary and finished by slamming his forehead over and over into the inert body under him. A bar boy appeared at his side with a schooner of dark beer, and the older man raised up like a lord, bloody and spent over his opponent. I thought, something has been settled here, finished for now. The younger man didn't move and lay in his own blood, and men stepped over him, and one toed the loser's outstretched arm back against his body to make more room. After a while the defeated young man moaned and rolled face down as if protecting his vitals too late and lay still again. Sometime later he got away or someone pulled him off to the side. I didn't see what happened. The lanterns hanging from the rafters moved the shadows in noticeable circles making me see the room shift and vibrate while I pretended to study my beer. The beer was weak and ill made, no longer German made, watered maybe by the owner and turned from good graciousness of hops into drunk-water. I had learned quickly not look right at anyone since the eye-to-eye contact always seemed to enrage, like looking directly at a bear. I tried to recall the fighters' faces, their nationality, but what I had seen blurred against the orange light.

I had been in Cincinnati only a matter of months, drinking my weak beer of initiation, and the matter of luck occurred to me. Suddenly one night during a fight like the one I just told about, maybe it was that one, but afterwards I remember thinking how the whole business of luck seemed to be much more vital in my new country. At any second, some straw driven on a wind could pierce your eye or lead you to gold. The story of a man in California being directed by a forked stick to a vein of gold in a hillside was current in the bar. He rounded a corner in a trail and the stick lay like an arrow in front of him urging him to look up at the rock wall. The vein of gold ore caught the light, the story went, like the finger of God showing the man his fortune. He spent only weeks then unloading God's grandeur with his pick and mining pan, bagging up the gold and hauling it to San Francisco. I heard a man tell this story with great reverence, and slowing near the end like a preacher coming to his exemplum, the man, not so old but

worn already as a stone is worn smooth by water, the man
raised his right hand, palm out and declared for the love of
luck. He said, "I think a man has to go where luck will find
him." And he looked into the eyes of his audience around
the table, men drinking Cincinnati. "I think a man has to
see the forked stick showing him the way and then go that
way. I find no forked sticks around here, boys. I can't see
the indicators no more in Cincinnati. Maybe they're here,
and I just can't see where they are. Maybe you boys can.
All's I know is: no forked sticks for me here."

He got up slowly from the table, his hand still raised
like a final benediction and then wheeled and walked out
the door. The men at the table sat quietly until he was
gone, no one daring to break the silence for mere trivia.
They waited and drank their beer. Finally, one man got up
and announced he had to pee, and the conversation
returned to wise cracks and women and money business.

After Germany, Cincinnati was as plain as a slice of
bread. Living there was like going back in time to a
Germany in the 14th century. Three or four hundred years
would be about right—water, sewers, manners were all
lacking. But space, opportunity, a small population, a
worker's value—these were gifts I couldn't have
understood sitting in a *Bierstube* in the old country. A good
worker in America has real value though the bosses pit us
against each other saying there's plenty more men who will
do my job if I won't; the pay is take it or leave it. That's at
first. Once you prove your worth, then the bosses begin to
compete for your labor, pay more, flatter you. They know

that the raw labor coming in from the East is really raw—
language raw, wanderlust raw. Every man without a wife
has his nose pointed towards tomorrow, something else,
something better and shinier. Every man alone is fragile on
the job, as likely to take off with the squeak of an attractive
rumor as to spit. Rumors: free land, gold, Indian women as
many as you want, beaver pelts stacked up waiting for
whiskey in trade, mountains a man can't get out of his mind
ever, steaming hot landscapes where a man can soak his
bones in the middle of a raging snow storm, so much land
you can't even imagine the edge of it.

With a wife, it's a different enterprise. The wives keep
men pointed toward something, it seems. The women
make men say what they're going to do and then hold them
to it, or explain why. And once the men say where they're
going, what they'll do there, they begin to believe it
themselves. In Cincinnati the West gets tried out. It was
still easy to go back. And anyway, the real West was not
there, not the West I got to know later. St. Louis was the
next place a man alone or a family could try out the idea of
the West. After that, the real thing happened to you like a
rainstorm happens to you. You could look for shelter and
ride out part of it, but the sure thing was that you'd get the
weather all over you sooner or later.

The brewery business in Ohio was not sewn up as tight
as it had been in Germany. But territory was clearly staked
out, and if you had a notion to fight someone for a piece of
the business, they would come after you as if you were
stealing their chickens. I learned that from Cleveland in the

north to Cincinnati in the south, all the big markets were taken. A man could find a small town and start brewing, but if he wanted to ship his beer out of town, he'd find plenty of thugs and scofflaws in the pay of the big brewers who would wreck his wagons and beat up his drivers and dump his beer in a field. A new brewer had to learn his place and then slowly and cautiously expand where he was allowed—new settlements, wedding parties. Slow was the word. Take what they give you, was the rumor in the brewery among those thinking of moving out on their own. Indiana was not far, but the conditions were the same. Go slow. Keep your head down and don't look the big brewers straight in the eye, or they'd feed you to their hogs.

On the other hand, if a man wanted to go off to the Dakotas among a mostly immigrant population, he could try anything and see what would happen. But the Dakota winters were the stuff of legends. And the Norwegians and Germans already there kept close company with their own kind. Some Russians and Canadians and Irish had set up too and sometimes would take in a new German or Bohemian as a brewer. Some men at the Koehler thought they'd point toward the Dakotas and see what happened. If it didn't work out, they could come back, not so far distant as you'd break anything getting back. Once you went through the Rockies, the coming back got much harder, the commitment of time and money greater, especially for families. A single man could exhaust his resources and then live off game or even stealing for a while until he decided to work again.

After two years in Cincinnati, I needed to find more signs. I found Fort Vancouver in the Oregon Territory. Later, how I got there.

The brewery in the fort kept the soldiers drunk and not much else. The owner, Meunch, had recently found that as he put it, "my guts feel like they want to eat me up." He walked around with his hand shoved in his shirt as if keeping all his gold there. But his eyes got tighter and deeper every day I worked for him. I knew he was storing up the pain each day like salt. Between rages at his workers, he sat exhausted at a desk overlooking the brewing process. His equipment was old and strung together like bad barbed wire. Hoses were spliced and filthy. He had a metal hygrometer the likes of which I hadn't seen except in history-of-brewing museums. Whatever he produced, the soldiers drank because they had no alternative. There was better beer forty miles south but no access for the soldiers.

I went to work for Meunch early in the fall of 1859 and by the beginning of winter, his face had turned as did the leaves to a yellow sere. He walked bent over to absorb the pain like a bullet in the guts. He went to see a doctor in Portland and came back grim and yellow with some powders to take that made him fall asleep. He was asleep even talking to you as the thing inside him ate and ate. I knew it would be weeks, and he could be dead. So I gathered all the money I had saved in Cincinnati, nearly $800, and began looking for a partner to supply the rest to buy out Meunch. I found a man not far away with the same idea and the same resources I had. And this man had the fortunate name of Bottler, George Bottler, who longed to fulfill some kind of name destiny and own a brewery. I had my training and brewing skills, Bottler his money and connections in Portland. Our plan was to buy out the Fort Vancouver brewery and move what was salvageable to Portland and then sell beer, better beer, back to the fort soldiers by the barrel barged out the Willamette River. The fort would be our first customers until we established the Portland market. I was so young that I couldn't even conceive of the Portland establishment, what structure and resistance they had already, the circles inside the inner circles. The western version of what I had left behind in Germany—long established deals and implicit agreements in place of open markets, skullduggery and collusions done with nothing more than a glance across a room. Now that I have come through these, I think that I should have known. How innocent I was. How young and German in a land where the English and Scots had founding roles and then could decide who else got to play.

Chapter Four

The Dogs of Portland

Portland, my first time, was an affair of dogs. There were dogs everywhere, allowed like revered beings to come and go in stores and streets and houses as if they were about some sacred missions. Dogs of no particular breeding, dogs of no particular grace, they were mostly brown dogs of small stature and flat heads. Had some master dog bred all these creatures? Why did so many of them look alike? I remember thinking the dogs of Cincinnati were as different from each other as wild flowers and were accorded no particular privilege either in the streets or houses. They were as likely to earn themselves a kick in the ribs as a scrap of food. They slunk along buildings and backdoors worrying the garbage, occasionally with a nose caught in a can by the ragged metal.

But in Portland, they were minor gods like Hindu monkeys. I tried to think why and couldn't. I asked a man on the mud street who had just thrown a crust of bread to a brown dog with four white feet, thinking it might be his dog or known to him.

"Fine looking dog," I said, not wanting confrontation, just access to the mystery.

"I suppose so," he said with no real conviction.

"Your dog?"

"Nope. Just a dog, I guess."

"Say, I'm from up at Fort Vancouver and haven't been down here before this. I wonder at all the dogs in Portland."

"German, you gotta be. Or a Swede. We get a lot of you people now, not so many before."

"Ya, German."

"Looking for work in the woods like the others? We get some Germans and Swedes working in the woods with the Finns."

"No, I'm a brewer. But about the dogs. I noticed that people here seem to be pretty nice to the dogs. Different from where I was last, in Cincinnati or even up at the fort in Vancouver where they don't put up with dogs much."

The man looked me over for a minute, maybe to see if I was worthy of his explaining time, maybe to see if I was a good German or a bad German. Finally, he explained. "You see dogs here have it hard. Maybe two out of three dogs die from eating salmon. Don't know why the other ones don't die but they don't for some reason. They'll all eat a dead salmon like it was butter cake. But some of 'em dies, some of 'em don't. I can't say why. Nobody seems to know. My father said the first dogs they brought out in the wagon trains—the same thing. Two out of three died eating salmon. So they kept the ones that didn't and kept breeding 'em together. New breeds, especially hounds and bird hunters got real expensive. A guy had to keep 'em penned or tied up or like livestock. People weren't used to keeping dogs that way. Lots of 'em died. Those dogs just went for a dead salmon the first one they could get." He looked at me to see if I was appreciating his information. I nodded and smiled and nodded again. He went on, "So we all kind of let the survivors have their way. Dogs are good critters to have around if they're not biters or yappers, you know. They keep the lowlifes and Indians from sneaking up and stealing you blind. They chase rats. Most of these dogs here are somebody's dog—not mine. But they do their dog work for all of us. Once in a while you have to shoot one that's got rabies, of course." He was warming up now to the subject. "Then there's your fancy hunting dogs the rich men keep on leashes. Those get into the salmon and they're gonners sure. Not one in three there. Those go down like flies."

After a while, he ran out of information about the dog world of Portland and got onto Germans. He said he knew of two kinds of Germans—the loggers and the fishermen. He didn't reckon he knew of brewers. I knew I was home.

I could move my brewery six blocks from the river and be on the edge of the woods. Six more blocks and the land was even cheaper, and access to river shipping just about the same.

The river is everything in Portland. The sharp outhouse smell in Cincinnati has been avoided here because the city fathers used the river water as city water in the beginning. Front street just up from the river is stacked with barrels and sacks at the mercantiles. Cut lumber you can smell but not see; the smell is coming from across the river at the sawmill, and the lumber is barged across when needed or loaded on ships bound outward toward the Columbia and then the Pacific. On milling days you can smell flour in the air arriving on the north wind from Spaulding's Mill.

The sun is just risen and one barge is coming slowly from upstream to tie up at the public docks, probably from Oregon City loaded with wheat and wool from south in the Willamette Valley. The falls there has created an industry of teamsters to haul produce around the cataracts and reload it on barges for Portland.

The warehouses on Front Street have a temporary look to them. The river comes up in the spring regularly to flood Front and even First and Second Streets, so the goods are never stored there permanently. I watch as the barge pulls in. No one else is up yet.

Two of the bargemen are French and chatter to each other in French. The third and fourth men are westerners with felt hats that seem formed by clouds or bird flight. It is May and rain is coming certainly before noon. The sky seems to lift with the arrival of the light, but I can see the clouds are just barely above the hills. The barge ties up and sets in motion the morning on the river.

The Willamette is high but behaving itself. A woman badly dressed comes from behind a Front Street building selling something from a basket covered in flour sackcloth. I am watching my new hometown show me what it's made of. I am thinking I will own this world, this light, soon

28

enough. I am wrong but smitten with possibility and a young man's delight in his own eyeballs seeing.

A woman has a basket and approaches the dock. She gives away samples. Two French men buy what look like buns. Now the carts are coming out, some empty and some laden with sacks. There seems to be some agreement about who can stack what where on the public docks. The stacking stops at an arbitrary, for me anyway, line that separates public from private spaces. Mud covers the planks laid to keep the carts from sinking out of sight. And men are mud from the calves down. There's a barge coming across the river from the east side with livestock—cattle and horses—penned precariously against the side. It looks heavy on one side, and the bargemen all stand leaning out on the high side for balance as it comes to the docks. With the river high there's a scramble to tie up before the whole shebang caroms off back into the heavy current. The Frenchmen watch listlessly, even contemptuously, picking their teeth and discussing something at length.

The signal somehow seems to have been given and the docks now fill up with calls and jostling for position. The line between public and private holds perfectly at the north end of the dock. There is clearly some kind of agreement in force. I suspect it has to do with money and property rights. My travels across the West from Cincinnati taught me about the power of free land and the competition for it; in one version or another, that's why all of us came to America—free land or its equivalent. There is apparently no free land on the Portland docks. It's all regulated by something I can't see, but I can see the results of the regulation. Now the animals come. Dray horses, teamster wagons creaking onto the docks, two hobbled brown milk cows looking terrified and being driven toward the ferry by a young boy in rags, now there are steaming piles of manure to step around. I'm gauging my new hometown. How quickly will the manure be carried away? What civil force is in charge of the manure? In Cincinnati, the Germans not only scooped up the manure with great aplomb but then made the manure available for city gardens—highly organized. In Portland, I watched to see where the manure would go. It went into the river. Six blocks from the river there were bears, six blocks from these civic docks the Indians and bears and deer owned the woods' darkness, its soft duff and deep velvet moss. Portland was beginning to feel for itself in the 1860s. The city felt as young in years as I was just breeching my thirties, heeding the song of this place—water and wood and raw humans thirsty for my beer.

The docks by midmorning were a mercantile swirl. It was clear to me that there was very little loafing here. Even the Frenchmen eventually took to off-loading their river barge with help from day workers looking for meal money. From my vantage point there seemed to be a high seriousness to all this activity as if there were some dread necessity to keep moving, some sense that this movement today meant food immediately tomorrow, and the converse—no movement, no food. The world was being invented each second, and I could clearly hear the ticks of

the mechanism. In Germany as a brewing apprentice, all of
the apprentices were gathered in the first days and made to
look at the works of an old cuckoo clock with its carved
wooden gears, weights, ratchets and levers. This is beer,
you are looking at, I remember our teacher telling us. All
the pieces are connected by necessary, calculated and
imperative links. It works because it has been thought out
for hundreds of years, and all the knowing is present in its
wheels and arrangement. This is beer, he repeated. Beer
has this arrangement too and will insist on being organized
in just one way—the correct way. I can still hear Herr
Grau's voice, see his finger in the air stirring our minds and
then pointing to the clock lying open before us like a
cadaver for medical students. The clock is beer; beer is a
clock.

The docks by noon are grinding on. Men are eating
and working side by side. The woman and her basket of
buns from the morning are long gone. The Frenchmen
have gone back across the river with new cargo. I am still
sitting watching my new town and planning to fill it with
beer—good beer. There will be no watering of my beer. I
want to control both the making and the shipping. The
selling will do itself once they taste good beer in Portland.
They have become used to bad beer at a high price. I will
bring them good beer at a low price.

Corbett mercantile has filled most of the non-public
side of the dock, and now all these goods are being carted
into his warehouse, the warehouse closest to the docks.
How fragile are these buildings if the river comes up

higher? I will have to ask with what frequency the river breaches its banks and enters the warehouses. The flourmill to the north sits on higher ground, I noticed. In my apprenticeship, we studied the rivers of Germany, the water of Germany, memorizing names and sources of rivers and which ones came from the mountains, which collected the dreck of cities, which passed through forests and what happened to the water. Water we studied long before we really studied beer. The water we began with determined the quality of the beer we would end up with. This river passing through Portland was significant: they got their drinking water from it not ten miles upstream. There were still outbreaks of typhoid until the turn of the century—the story of water was the story of the West.

The day I stood watching the docks in Portland, I counted nine dead cats, four dead dogs, five dead sheep and what looked to have been a goat on my walk to the river. I was walking around the long way from the rooming house to see what the streets were like. I think, as in most western towns, that the people thought something would drag the dead things away and eat them. But the carcasses lay in the spring rain puddles and these became thick with a kind of oil slick that dead things produce, some essential part of the creature rendered off first before the bloating and maggots. In Cincinnati there had been a city worker whose job it was to collect the dead things. After crossing the Mississippi River, I never found a single instance of this civic carcass collecting. The dead things, it was assumed, would return to the earth or be eaten on the spot. A dead horse would be dragged away from the front of a dry goods store or a saloon, but smaller critters lay where they fell. When I reached the docks, my inventory of the dead complete, I found no dead things at the docks. Either they had been removed or dumped into the river. I was looking for good water sources earlier in the day, I remember, and thinking how much work would have to go into reducing turbidity before I could use the water for beer. A glass of water in 1865, left standing for ten minutes, would precipitate out a solid cover for the bottom of the glass. I knew I would need multiple sand filters before the water was worth the brewing effort. You couldn't cover bad water with good brewing; but you could make bad water drinkable. The dead creatures and garbage in the streets all ran into the river and headed for the Columbia River and eventually the sea. I would have to keep an eye on upstream development where my water would originate.

The docks filled and cleared, filled and cleared of barrels, spools of hemp rope, animals, sacks of flour, boxes and bags and crates—the desideratum of civilization. By late afternoon barges came from the south with produce from the Willamette Valley—flax and wool from Salem, wheat for Spaulding's mill coming in from all over the valley, and small bales of hops from Independence and as far up river as Eugene. I spotted the tell-tale green of the hops immediately. The bales had come in alongside root vegetables, and I knew it was too early in the growing season for these to be this year's crop. Every household had a hops plant or two all across the West growing up on the porch or an arbor in a garden. Besides beer, hops were a favorite blood medicine and gave favorable results in administering to all sorts of intestinal complaints from one end to the other. These hops were poor green for beer, but good for compounding medicines. Still my beer-maker's heart quickened at the sight of them there next to spring beet greens and young carrots. The vegetable loveliness of the whole business allowed me to see into the future. I knew I could make my beer here in Portland.

The money in 1865 in Portland followed strictly regulated paths, not regulated by any government, but touching a certain number of hands before it could work its way into the community. A bank owned by Henry Winslow Corbett, William Ladd and Henry Failing and their associates was always a good vehicle for introducing money into town, making it legitimate and fair currency. Eventually these gentlemen owned not only the best real estate in town, but the drinking water as well. So they were already partners in my beer without knowing it. I put $800 in their bank to let them know that I was present in town and seeking my fortune with their permission. Banking was a gentleman's profession in the West as well as the East. A man didn't have to dedicate too much time to the banking business if he could just start up and get the trust of the community. Real estate—land in every sort and size, every deal and shared deal—now that took time and cultivation. Banking was just keeping good records and finding trustworthy people: women were the best at both. If you could find good women to keep records for you, they would act as insulation against greedy and ambitious men employees. With land you had try to predict where the people would settle, or you had to make sure they'd settle where you owned. I knew I didn't want to try the land game in Portland with my German accent, at least not until I got some good people around me. My accent, I learned, announced me as a logger or a river boatman. My clothes had to say I was neither. I dressed as finely as a man would dare in a frontier town according if not distinction then confusion to my encounters with the tribes that ruled money and land.

I was sure of one thing: that the English left to their own devices could not come up with a decent beer to save their miserable existences. Neither could the Scots. I also knew from Cincinnati that an English, Irish or Scotsman would smack his lips and roll his eyes when he did encounter a fine beer, a beer he was simply not capable of making himself.

By evening I had done my count of dead animals, my survey of dock activity morning and afternoon, and my search for high ground and good water in my new hometown. I calculated that I'd need a good brick building to do my warm-side, cool-side magic: warm for the making, cool for the storage. In the winter I'd want the southern sun to come in the high windows and cook the damp out of the building. In the summer I'd want the overhead sun deflected off the roof and away from the windows to keep the cool side cool. I went looking for bricks. After the Civil War there would be a number of fine Negro brick

makers in the valley, men who had learned their trade
working for some southern master and had taken their
trade west. But before and during the war, brick making
was often done by amateurs who had seen someone else do
it and had the good fortune to find a vein of useful clay in a
riverbed on their property. The business of finding good
brick, when I first came into Portland, was a miserable one
consisting of gathering rumors and hearsay and then cross-
checking one against the other, then going to look where
good brick had been reported, then finding and making a
deal with the manufacturer. Three times I found a single
man making bricks as fast as he could using his children
and wife as labor. The bricks disappeared as fast as he
could make them. There was no stockpile to buy from,
nothing but a promise about next month or come summer
or, once, "if the river stays its banks." Finally I found a
young German who also did not fit the standard of river-
German or woods-German. He had three men working
for him using clay shipped by the river from south in the
Willamette Valley near the settlement of Monroe. Monroe,
it seemed, could not use all the clay it had, though a
substantial brick-making endeavor was under way there. I
had found my bricks and in good quantity and sufficient
number, so I could plan for my future brewery building.

In less than a year Bottler and I had a brewery, not with
new bricks yet but in an old warehouse on First and Davis
along the river. We brought in water and filtered it
ourselves through various layers of sand, as I had been
taught in Germany. We had no proprietary spring as the

best breweries in the old country would; we had water that needed to be brewed into existence. I never drank any of the so called "drinking water" of the city of Portland until after the turn of the century, many years later. The river water was subject to dead animals, human waste—the same ravages and corruption I had seen on the city streets. My job—my calling and mission--would be to make this water safely into beer inside my temple of bricks. Within that first year we failed at the river front brewery. Many reasons, mostly Bottler, but I needed his money. Another year later Bottler and I were gathering bricks again from my German to build a brewery on 12th Street up the hill and away from the river. It was better to make beer away from the river, I had learned.

One conversation with George Bottler went something like this:

"Henry, if you would let me buy the hops and yeast, I think I could do better than you do because they always try to cheat people with a German accent. The belief is that Germans are...well, stupid. There is something about the accent that encourages people to think that way. I know you are not stupid, that Germans as a group are not stupid, but I'm just saying the guttural comes off less intelligent in English than it does in German. Hold your horses, Henry. Hold your horses. It's not your fault. It's not *anybody's* fault, really. That's just the way things are. Now your Frenchman's accent sounds pretty good in English. Just a little hard to figure out what he's saying, but the sound's pretty good. At least he doesn't sound stupid, if you know what I mean."

I will relate neither what I was saying, nor what I was thinking. I just want you to appreciate what I had to listen to from Bottler for nearly a year.

"So Henry, I think you have a hard row to hoe in the marketplace, if you get my point. In my acquaintance, your German in Portland will be in the beer business—retail— or work in the woods. Some on the boats too, of course. And most stay with their own kind, speaking their German, eating German, being German except in the United States of America. Most of you Germans think German things are the best, but, by God, you people have to look up and see where you find yourself these days—here, not Germany. And for damn good reasons you're here. Because the old world is one hell of a failure. That's why we're all here, for that matter. It gets stuck in my craw, that nostalgia for an Old World that never existed, never in a million years."

George got going very easily and had a hard time stopping once he got wound up. He seemed to goad himself to higher and higher bombast as if some fierceness of brain had lambasted all his other senses. He was mostly a reasonable man but subject to fits of passion and intransigent positions. He was not a debater but layer on of diatribe.

"The Old World, indeed. Worn out economies and worn out creeds. The Scotch now, they'll haul back their money at the slightest grumble in the economy of the West.

38

Lord Airlie and the Dundee bankers yank back on the money the second one of their flunkies gets the collywobbles. And your Irishman is just sort of low-grade Englishman, after all is said and done. Who the hell can tell them apart once they spend ten years in America. I knew an Englishman who said he could spot the Irish at one hundred paces. Something about the way they carried their hands—not quite up to civilization yet and not likely to fake it very well. I don't know."

Now there was something you rarely heard from George—I don't know. I tried to get him to say it again as a kind of confirmation, but I couldn't lead him back to it. I don't believe I ever heard him say it again in our association.

"So my good Weinhard, where was I? Oh there. We try to put them all together out here, but really they don't mix except when it's a matter of economic convenience. Like you and me, Henry. We respect each other and have come together seeking mutual benefit in this beer business. That will be enough in the long run, I think."

Bottler and I had lasted less than six months on the river front location. I went back temporarily to brewing at the fort, and Bottler moved into small buildings as the City Brewery on Burnside. I ended up buying out Henry Saxer's Liberty Brewery, eventually owning George's brewing capacity too, and having Portland to myself by 1864. Not too bad for a boy from Wurttemberg. I never missed working for someone else. I fit the position of boss as if I had trained for it all my life. Bottler had one more thing to say.

"When the time comes, Henry, you and me will be the men who own the West. We take chances and reap the rewards. That's the key thing: stick your neck out and take the chance. We're the ones, Henry. You and me."

As I said, I had to listen to George for less than six months and then only briefly a few years later when I bought him out and sent him on his way. He was a westerner through and through—enthusiasm and opinion abounding. Skill, education, discipline and perspicacity were what he lacked. The story of the West: new people finding new solutions to old problems that had already stalled Europe hundreds of years ago. I knew enough German history to know that free land would not be the solution to all of Europe's problems.

Chapter Five

Wurttemberg, Germany

Wurttemberg, town of Lindenbronn, Germany, 1850: I was twenty years old and committed to brewing as a recession-proof livelihood. I would be a professional, go as far as I could without owning my own brewery, never quite be a burgher. What kind of thing drives a man to leave his hometown and family and go to a place about which he knows nothing more than rumor and innuendo, about which there is no hard information but tales and lies? It would be like entering a fairy tale, sucked through the pages of the book and finding oneself surrounded by the drawings of the tale, at the whim of the illogic of the storyteller's artful fiction. I try to remember what enticed me into the story of America.

The Indians, of course. Where in Europe was such color and wild excitement? Where was a natural man in all of Europe? There were stories of boys raised by wolves, of course. There were the Russian Cossacks. The wild men of Borneo. But the American Indians had, in the stories, all the style of nature herself: of hurricanes and floods and plagues and thunderstorms. They took scalps, we heard—such perfectly elegant if diminutive barbarism.

But stories of America were only one draw. In the late 1840's in Wurttemberg, everywhere in Germany, Austria and Prussia actually, there were insurrections, uprisings against the old aristocrats and the kings. And like all disturbances of this sort, they were expensive, and the *Kleinburgers*, the little people, were the first to suffer. I had gone to Stuttgart to brew beer and study the brewer's trade. My home town of Lindenbronn was peaceful and a delicious place to grow up. But soon the hills felt like they were binding me to the earth, and apprenticing in the breweries would give me a bigger sky. And it was during my apprenticeship that the uprisings occurred. Many of the King's troops defected to the side of rebellion and personal freedoms. But the powerful Prussian army was called in by Frederick of Wurttemberg and his oldest brother, the King of Prussia made sure little Frederick did not lose the battle. These were bad times—the Austrians were vicious in their reprisals against soldier deserters, the Prussians were stupid and heavy handed and reactionary as usual, and we poor Swabians were left holding our hands out and pleading with the aristocracy not to take our land—pleading for our miserable jobs. In '46 the potatoes failed, then quickly after, the other grains. The Prussians, blunt instruments that they are, rejected railroad building and retreated to their intellectual caves and the great make-work projects of connecting German cities and regions all stopped. These were bad times to be anywhere in the German-speaking world. America beckoned not like a siren but like a delicious adventure. It was the room, yes. But it was also

42

the paucity of rules. We read about America that they were making up the rules as they went along each day. Everything was allowed unless it was obviously stupid or venially evil. The rest was negotiable.

In Lindenbronn my mother understood, my father didn't. We were, my father said, the recipients of thousands of years of trial and error at the business of civility. We had many rights in the Wurttemberg region that others didn't have—property was the most important, always property. Then we had a regional parliament that made sure all the property holders were heard no matter how low on the social scale. This was unique in Wurttemberg. My mother rolled her Swabisch eyes toward the heavens because my father was off on his historical lesson on the genius of the Swabisch people: civil structure, universities, food cleanliness, self-maintenance. I dreamed of a gathering storm on the American prairie. Wurttemberg region was packed with breweries. America would be packed with something else, something I couldn't quite imagine. But there would be Indians and immense storms that would fill the sky with black thunderheads and lightning would rain out of them flashing like the eyes of God—Lutheran God—who had given up on the Old World and now had cast his lot with the New World. My mother rolled her eyes again. She could sign her name (for church and civic registries) but that was the extent of her literacy. But her sense of the grand adventure of America was extraordinarily accurate.

"Find out what's there and tell us. We might give up everything and come over too," she said and dug my father in the ribs knowing he would rise to the occasion.

"On the contrary," he began. She had set him up. "Modern German speakers are experiencing the height of civilized Europe. There is no language like our German, the Swabisch dialect aside. It is the reason we are held together."

He was no German nationalist, but he believed all the German speakers sharing the glory of the German language were linked up by a common duty, a common responsibility—to use German correctly and speak as an example to others. Say the words properly. Finish the syllables. Construct your sentences with the correct succession of tenses.

As he spoke his words became more and more distinct, more boldly spoken until he arrived at ersatz theatrical. My mother, having set him off, would nod and smile and encourage his raving for as long as she could. I once asked her when he wasn't present why she did that.

"What?" she posed innocently. "Whatever could you possibly mean?" And she rolled her eyes, put both hands together on the side of her face—angelic—and laughed. I looked askance. "Oh that. That is a game I have played with your father since we were first married."

"But it looks to me only one of you is really playing, mother. He doesn't seem to be aware of what you're doing."

"I used to think so. Now I'm not so sure. Sometimes I think he knows exactly what I'm doing. And so he pretends to be what I want him to be, maybe to please me. Maybe just to play back. Now I'm not sure any more who is playing what. It's just something we have always done—I goad him and he goes. Anyway, we both like it, so what does it matter."

My mother laughed: at my father's seriousness, at her Swabian world of duties and obligations. But she also served both masters while laughing at them. It was a beautiful balancing job. I was old enough to appreciate the whole business by the time I left for America. On the matter of going to America my father made it clear that I was of an age to do what I wanted, but I would be giving up citizenship in a civilized country for pipe dreams and a fool's errand and *dumheit*—foolishness. And then the potato failure, the grain failures, the insurrection failures, the parliamentary failures. The Austrian reprisals, the Prussian ruthlessness…and I think finally, at the end before I was to go to America, he thought maybe I was doing the right thing. The Wurttemberg world was rattling as if an earthquake were shaking it apart. At the end, only the Swabisch brewing world held steady. Hops were sometimes excellent, sometimes only acceptable, but never failed as the potatoes had. Beer didn't fail; governments and ideologies failed. By the time of my leaving, Karl Marx was agitating in Dusseldorf, Friedrich Engles in Ebberfeld, and Moses Hess in Cologne. Something large was looming in the German labor market, something ominous in the diets. And I had turned my head and all that was in it toward America.

In Portland politics and economics seemed much simpler than in Wurttemberg. In Portland they were the same thing. It was the frontier simplicity—the complicated (in Europe) was always collapsing into simpler forms in the West. There was a United States government, but it was far away and its representatives largely absent. There was a state government up river in Salem, but its machinations were pale reflections of Portland's needs. Portland barked and the tail would wag in Salem.

My first unsuccessful year in Portland brewing with George Bottler was an initiation of sorts. Let me show you.

We had opened our doors in a warehouse on First and Davis Streets—too close to the river I felt, but the rent was cheap. If the river came up, we could lose everything if it came too fast. The building didn't have a warm side and a cool side as I thought it should in ideal circumstances. The heat from the brewing kettles leaked unimpeded into barrel storage side. It was like brewing in a home cellar—no controls, no discipline, no rigor. We were making food in a kind of gutter. We trucked the water in from Oregon City and filtered it through three layers of sand. If Bottler had had his way, we would have slurped water directly out of the Willamette River, let the sediment swirl to the bottom and made beer with what was left. We began to part ways immediately, never mind the dumb-German-accent business he insisted on, assuming for himself the business

46

front position. For me the beer-making was everything. But like my mother's saving grace humor, America had assumed a comic overcast. I could laugh at it all and keep my distance while engaging the brewing and money worlds with the high seriousness my father affected. I considered myself well armed for the vicissitudes in Portland.

During my time with Bottler I had occasion to fall back on the twin pillars of character from my mother and father. George Bottler was a man of potent eyebrows. What I mean by that is he used his eyebrows to intimidate people as a large man might use his size, a witty man his wit. His eyebrows were entities that he must have confronted every day in the mirror so that I imagine him practicing the raising and lowering, first one then the other then both together, the darkening glare with both creatures lowered across hooded eyes as if small dangerous dogs were arching their backs on his behalf. I actually saw George in a conversation with a hops seller adjust his eyebrows both at once with a quick swipe of two moistened index fingers against the grain. The result was a startling bushiness that seemed to pierce the heart of his adversary's arguments and reluctance. The eyebrows bristled and the man was George's.

After his eyebrows, there was much less to George than met the eye. His many chins bragged of his habits at table, his thinning hair was always behaving badly no matter how recently clipped, his suits betrayed his undisciplined flesh beneath, and his sausage fingers seemed to be cooking and plumping with the heat of him. He stood too close when he talked to you. I would step back, and he would advance. If I walked around, he followed, always coming inside my German-guarded space and distance so that I found myself constantly retreating in his presence. I needed him, I thought, as a partner and representative in the community. I should have chosen another German, a Jew from southern Germany preferably, because I could have been sure of what I was not sure of with George—intelligence and German discipline. I was young and let George seduce me with his powerful eyebrows, and I paid for it.

George loved to drink beer, so I thought he'd make a good partner in brewing. He had been engaged with Meunch in Fort Vancouver, so I thought he knew what he was doing (although in retrospect, the bad beer of Meunch's brewery should have tipped me off to that partnership). I plead my youth and inexperience, but I don't let myself off the hook so easily. Writing now from old age I can see clearly my follies. In fact what's most interesting to me looking back over my life is where I failed. The successes were many, finally. I don't remember them in detail; they seemed rather to accumulate than occur. The failures, though, those stand out clearly. The West was very good to me in that way. I now delight in how I responded to the kicks in the butt my new country meted out, how clearly those kicks directed my attention to the business of becoming an American.

George was a good lesson and, in retrospect, easily learned. Not cheap though. I found myself failed in Portland and back at Fort Vancouver working for Meunch with the daily prospects of batch after batch of mediocre to poor beer. I knew what we were doing to make bad beer: poor sterilization so wild yeasts got in, put in kegs green and over or under sugared, barrels of immature wood still seeping sap into the beer (this a crime of short cut, not ill-discipline like the others). Even so, as long as the beer had alcohol in it, the soldiers didn't seem to mind. Meunch was becoming more ill by the week, the pain now his constant companion, filling him so that his eyes seemed to send the pain out in his squint. He wandered his brewery as if looking for something there that would make the hurting stop. I think he knew what was happening and how long he might hold out. But he had nothing else to do: his wife patiently fed him and tried to get him to sleep. His workers waited a death-watch like cattle waiting to leave a dying cowboy. My role in this business of finality was to assure Meunch that his wife would have enough money to move back to her people in Saint Louis, and then I could take what equipment was left after paying his wife and do whatever I wanted with the brewery.

Meunch's skin became ashen and paper-thin. If he bumped a fence rail he would bleed and the torn skin would flap from his hand. He bandaged it back on and went about his business. Toward the end he had the look of a battlefield refugee and even began to walk hunched against the pain, carrying it like a weight against his hip. He was taking some potions concocted by a Chinese man who sometimes cooked at the garrison. After taking the potion he would seem to recover briefly, straighten up, and then slowly slide back to where he was, and then back further to worse yet.

One day I found Meunch sitting on a bale of hops staring off to somewhere on the horizon. I asked him if he was feeling bad.

"Not very bad, no, thank you, Henry. Just today the pain has rounded out onto itself somehow. It's like part of it is working to cancel some other part. And I feel a little better. But the light. Look at it there in the West. It's like you could pick it up and put it in a sack if you wanted. It suddenly seems to have a kind of heft to it, thickness, you know. I don't know why." He looked away from me and back to the horizon as if despairing of making me understand. "I'm not a man of fancy words, Henry, but suddenly I feel the need for every word I ever heard to get the telling done. The saying is very important. My poor wife has had to listen to me try to say what I was trying to say. It seems so important now. So important finally to say all the things I didn't say before, like about the light. I never said much about the light before."

I hadn't met a dying man like this one (and Mr. Els, later) before, not in Germany, not in coming across America. I thought about what to say and couldn't find anything. I thought about the coyotes I had seen.

There were so many coming across the West that people had stopped shooting at them.

Meunch picked at the hops bale and crushed some under his nose and breathed in the aroma. "It's funny. Almost. I look at the light every time of day, not just sunrise and sunset. And then I smell the things around me at the same time as if I'm trying to live the rest of my life quickly before it finishes. I find myself wishing I had been doing this all along. And then I realize I couldn't do this without seeing the end so clearly."

We spoke German, and I couldn't get the coyotes out of my mind. They would come into camp low and friendly like masquerading dogs, as if maybe we wouldn't recognize them if they were nice enough. Then someone would throw a rock at them, and they'd scatter into the sagebrush. Then in a comic repetition they'd do the same thing again until someone wasted a bullet on the lead coyote, and that would drive them all away for a while. It was the cooking that drove them crazy, the bacon and pork fat hitting the pan, the fresh game hanging, waiting to go into the pot.

Meunch fell silent as if refilling from the light and smell of hops. Then, finally, "Henry, this is what I came west for, this emptiness. It got so I couldn't stand to be around people anymore, first in Germany, then in the East of this country. Couldn't stand anyone but my wife after a while. I think at one point I could have gone off to the mountains to live on meat and leaves." He laughed. "But somewhere in every German is this other thing, this *gemutlich* lover. My gift is beer. Bad beer but beer just the same." I tried to protest that the beer wasn't really bad. It just needed a little more careful… "Ya, ya, ya," he said waving away imaginary lies from in front of his eyes. "Bad beer is bad beer. But unlike you, Henry, I didn't have the grand advantage of a Swabisch apprenticeship. I learned beer from an uncle who worked my ass off. My jobs in his brewery were anything that smelled bad, was repetitious, or dangerous. I was my father's gift to his brother. And my uncle's gift to me was going to be that I would learn a trade and to work like a man. So as soon as I thought I had the process down, I ran away to America with a stolen hygrometer. And I stole also a silver tray from my uncle's house, and that paid for my passage. I figured he owed me at least that much."

In the evening during my crossing, the coyotes surrounded us and sang to each other.

"So when I wrote my parents from America, they wrote back and disowned me for my theft. They made up the money to my uncle out of my sister's dowry, and, they said, she had to marry down instead of up. But I knew what my sister's face looked like when she was a young woman. I think that was the cause of her marrying down, not any dowry." Meunch laughed again then searched the light for signs of newness. I was beginning to feel split in two by my coyote remembering while Meunch talked about his life. And the more detailed he got—his sister, his father—the more my mind, on its own, roamed to coyotes and the crossing. I tried to concentrate on what Meunch was saying, but I was a young man, just barely a man, it seems to me now. And I remember thinking later that maybe the coyotes were my way of not having to deal with a man who was dying. Young men don't like to think about dying, find it almost constitutionally impossible. This is what has always made war possible—old men needing to twist the world to some defining shape before they die, young men incapable of distinguishing between adventure and the final greed of old men.

꙳ Meunch stood up, his hand in his jacket to hold the pain there for a moment. "Come Henry, I want to show you something." He walked slowly as if his shoes had become heavy. Around the side of the brewing shed were the remains of a wagon: boards shredded by worms, wheels just spokes with the iron gone, skeletal ribs of bows, tongue lolling out like a comic skull. He stood pondering the pile as if it were great art, looking for its meaning. Finally he said, "This, Henry, is how I got here to Fort Vancouver. The last part of it, anyway. My uncle was part of how I got here. King Fredrick of Prussia was part. My father, my German-ness, my great belief that anywhere would be better than staying home—these too got me here. But this wagon was the last part, down the Columbia River. I kept it here...I don't know why. I think maybe I thought I could go back as long as it was here. So I watched it rot every day, my way back, my last chance to call the whole thing off and go be a good German boy, my father's son. Finally I started to use parts of it for other things—the wheel iron, the wiffletree, the best wood."

Once, I think just out of where Nebraska is now, when we had started west, the coyotes seemed half tame and so used to people they would dart into the camp and try to snatch a young child as if it were just another herd animal. They must have had some success with this tactic in the past because they came in the evening over and over trying to pick off children. The men finally organized and hid under a wagon near the direction the coyotes came from, and were going to shoot every bold raider. The men waited for hours, but the coyotes had apparently called off the assault as soon as the men hid.

"The wagon was my way back to somewhere I didn't want to go, and when it collapsed I felt relieved, like a door shut and locked. Oh, I knew I could still catch a boat out of Astoria, San Francisco, then New York and finally home to Germany. I thought about it when I got this sickness. For just a second I imagined myself going home to die, being buried near my parents—my sister would do it out of duty. Then I imagined myself rotting in German soil with all the other Germans. Or I could be buried here near the Columbia River and my juices washing out to sea in the company of elk, bear, salmon, Indians and the odd wandering white man. My juices had chosen. When I am gone you will pay my wife a fair price for the brewery and then make good beer for the soldiers."

He seemed satisfied with his portrait of how things would be. His German had none of my southern softness. We Swabisch could tell what village you came from by your accent. Meunch spit when he talked. He seemed satisfied, made a gesture with the back of his hand to the pile of wagon orts, then walked off toward the house with his back straight.

Meunch was dead six weeks later. The genius of his brewery was not the beer, or even the water but that he never had to ship a drop anywhere but where it was made.

The soldiers at the fort drank all the bad beer he could produce. Very little was left over, and when there was and he tried to ship it even as close as up river to Portland, the beer went from bad beer to rotten beer. I don't know the English word for rotten beer, maybe undrinkable-even-by-a-thirsty-man.

The death of Meunch came after elaborate final gestures. There was no ritual of death for these new people in the West—none of home-country rituals seemed apt, not Scottish rite or English dirge, German somber or French insouciance. People in the West found death to be the singular most lonely proposition of the westering. There seemed to be the overwhelming sense that we are not in this together finally; one at a time we die. Meunch's wife Alice sought out the Indian doctors after all other forms of physician had failed and told her to prepare for his death. The first Indian man came reluctantly because, he said, Meunch had not lived on the sagebrush side of the mountains where the medicine man's power to heal came from. The sagebrush itself in varying potencies, burning bunches of grasses, concoctions of bone and earth and insects and wood shavings--all these and more in a tightly wrapped bundle plus the invoking of spirits—this was the medicine of final resort for Meunch.

The healer swept the room. Alice had somehow prevailed upon him to commence, no matter the possible lack of powers. Meunch was in such pain that it exhausted him, and he only occasionally came to be conscious of the pain until he slept again. The fort doctor had suggested to

Alice that she might try giving him whiskey toward the end, lots of whiskey to see him through the pain, but the whiskey produced such violent pain in his stomach that she quickly stopped. The Indian healer made a mash of sage and other things and when Meunch could get some down, he seemed to stay awake longer with less pain. The room smelled of sage as if it had been distilled from the air on some hot spring day when you breathed the bush in every lungful.

I came into the room from working the brewery and felt the thickness of the air. The Indian was sitting uneasily in a chair near the bed rubbing together threads of something and something else. Alice had dressed the windows in dark cloth to keep the light low so that the room seemed lit by a distant fire. Smoke hung in the middle of the room in a cloudbank. When I entered, the Indian moved away from the bed to a corner and sat on a gray blanket. He said nothing. I nodded to him and spoke some inanity to Meunch, but his eyes were closed, almost at peace. The furrowed brow etched by each day of pain had come to relax, and he looked years younger suddenly. He seemed self-contained to me, perfect unto himself, beyond Lutheran ritual or even the promise of salvation itself. I wanted to mutter some bible verse by way of benediction, something ready-made and pertinent, something so appropriate that it would contain, if only for a moment, his whole brewer's life. And, of course, nothing came in that firelight that wasn't firelight, that sickroom of melded cultures. When I didn't sit in the chair, the Indian retook his seat and continued to roll together threads. I thought that this was impossible anywhere but here in the American West. When the smoke leaked away, the smell of brewery mash regained the room. The Indian refilled the room with smoke from his newly rolled threads, first to the four directions and finally up, but not down. Meunch moved as if he was awake, but his eyes remained closed as if he'd had enough of seeing the world. I was young and shifted from one foot to the other feeling for what I should do. Many years later at the death of a friend I knew to feel what was there in the death, the loss and thoroughness of the finality. But in Meunch's last evening I felt my youth and its insufficiency, even its hollowness and inability to contain a death. I knew I owed him my solemnity, some ritual presence. But I was aware of part of myself curiously watching to see what would happen, what this business of death was like and what it had to do with me.

In Germany an uncle had died, no, was killed, in the insurrection of 1848. I was 18 and found that I could without effort hand over all my feelings and duties and even my very presence at the funeral to other agents: my parents, the ritual so certain of what to do with the occasion, the germanity of the food and proper words and gestures. I simply lifted my feet and was carried by everything around me. At Fort Vancouver the death of Meunch seemed hacked to pieces—Indian, Alice, the smell of brewing mash, the smoke curtain of sage. The pieces were all awkward banging into each other. And me. I finally sat on the bed and just waited until I thought I had waited long enough, until his breathing was even and seemed like sleep, whether it was or not. And then I stood and nodded to the Indian who was still busy with another preparation, I think. I left to walk out past Alice, through the living room and into an easy rain the thirsty earth absorbed immediately. I remember thinking that I was walking back into life from that room, that house. I know better now. I was in life in that room but didn't have the sense to watch it closely. Maybe that is the distillation of what the West has taught me: all of this is original, the first time—pay attention.

I made a deal with Alice a week after Meunch's death. With Bottler we had enough money to buy the brewery equipment. Part of it we took to Portland for our short-lived partnership. Part of it we left in Fort Vancouver, enough of it for my brief return. Eventually my second Portland brewery went so well that it surprised me, and my only job was to hang on while the business took off. I made good beer. That's the short of it. I made stable, consistent and flavorful beer the likes of which had not been tasted in the West. I began shipping up the coast, then down the coast and eventually to Russia, China and ports in between. The blur of success: a wise old man once told me he only remembered well in his life when he had failed at some enterprise or another; the successes all ran together without any real distinction. So beer was my first success. The girls were my second, but more later. The girls, and my love, ah my love.

Chapter Six

Joshua

I found myself right from the beginning in Cincinnati confounded by the American liberties taken with names and identities. Men and women changed names with ease and with the name changes came fabricated lives, adjusted histories, absolutions personally conferred, and then momentary identities made for the day, the moment. I tried it myself early on in my career in America. I called myself Heinrich, then Friedrich, then Otto and finally Johannes. I became emboldened when it didn't seem to matter what I claimed as a name and began to run through last names, some German, the some English and then just made-up names to see if there was any consequence. None. Then I began to assume all the people around me had claimed an equal state of flux and protean identities— procrustean beds to accommodate the new conditions of the new world. I returned to my real name when I got the job in the brewery because it matched the name on the German brewery league certificate. It was the Old World that had required that I be who I really was. Nothing in the New World required a constant identity. My German immigrant bosses recognized my Swabisch apprenticeship papers from Stuttgart; I became what the papers attested to.

I began to hear stories about the desperate with desperately concocted identities, men and women escaping the law for murder or significant robberies. Without national or regional identification papers or registries of any sort, America became a free-for-all of invention. Who should I be today? As long as I keep moving, I can be whatever I want today.

A clever young man, Joshua Aldridge was one of his names, began life somewhere on an upstate New York farm, left, it was said, with the first significant beating his father gave him, and looked west without ceasing. Along the way he became a doctor, a large-animal veterinarian, a dentist, a bridge-building engineer and a lawyer in a small town. The story of Joshua came to me from several sources—the men at the brewery, in which case the story took the flavor of a brothers Gimm tale as it was swept up in the German telling, and several nights in the bar where I learned most of my English, the story surfaced with significant variations in detail.

Joshua was an inventor of himself, and a facile—a quick learner who could approximate any skill he saw demonstrated. If he saw it he could do it. His secret was in the doing.

One version went that another of Joshua's secrets was that he always looked like what he was supposed to be. So, I guess, he was an actor of sorts. And everyone who had contact with him remembered him differently—his hair, his height, his weight, his eye color. No two descriptions matched, but it was always him, it turned out, always Joshua. And the problem with Joshua was that each invention in each place seemed to begin to define him for that place, and he eventually rebelled against being only that one thing for that one place. He was driven to move on by his need to change into something else, and America accommodated him by always having someplace else for him to go.

West was the obvious direction of accommodation. From Cincinnati where he was becoming in demand as a tooth puller, he was said to have taken to the legal profession just outside St. Louis. Then farther west he became a wagon-train guide, a railroad track engineer, a stockman for the railroads and finally a doctor again making his reputation with poultices learned from the Indians. Joshua, it occurred to me while drinking my beer and hearing yet another piece of his lore, had become an amalgamation, like beer, of local materials, and these materials were melted into, brewed, these stories of Joshua. I began to wonder at the popularity of the Joshua stories, whether the groups of people who told the stories were looking for something in their fascination with Joshua. Or was Joshua the essential ingredient? I took my whole life in the West to answer the question eventually.

One Joshua story went that he showed up in a town just outside St. Louis—some said the Illinois side of the river, some insisted it was still in Missouri. There had been a steamboat accident in which the boat ran aground on a sand bar and then the boiler exploded shooting people and freight and animals into the air and landing all three randomly in trees, on the dock and well into the streets of the sleepy town. Boys and dogs ran around yelping at the rain of bodies and cotton and hogs. Just when some of the bodies had been lined up in the dirt of the street, and some even still breathing, the wounded animals shot, and the civil order reestablished, Joshua appeared himself as if blown from the boat or dropped from the sky. He was wearing a vest and carrying a doctor's bag and began immediately to pass over the dead and dying with a professional touch pronouncing life here, death there. With the living he began to bandage and suture without a word, not answering inquiries about who he was except by his acts. Finally he spoke and instructed the townsfolk in propping and splinting and boiling rags for more bandages like a battlefield surgeon. When the carnage fell under his control, he spoke orders efficiently and even the local sawbones began to follow his instructions.

At the end, the dead were carted away to the cemetery. The living sheltered from the increasing heat of the day, the dogs shooed off the bloody clothing, the hog meat shared out among the citizens, a messenger sent down to St. Louis to inform the steamboat company—all were directed by the stranger in the vest. Said his name was Joshua. No one seemed to have caught the last name or a few heard different names at different moments during the excitement.

I heard this from a young man who had come to Cincinnati from St. Louis by river. He heard the story on the up-river ride. He said several other people chimed in once the teller got going as if they had only been waiting for the Samaritan tale to add what they heard too. The young man could only swear to what he'd heard and said he knew nothing first hand.

Several beers later another man from down river joined our table with his beer. He'd overheard the story of Joshua and wanted to add what he knew—the bad Joshua part—of the Joshua tale.

It happened farther west, somewhere up the Missouri River drainage toward Montana country, maybe just before Montana, the man said. It began with some kind of Indian swindle involving a half-barrel of whiskey that had a false bottom full of water so it hefted like it was full but was only really less than half whiskey. The Indians discovered the fraud and came looking for the trapper who had sold them the lame barrel. He was long gone, having understood from the beginning that his scheme depended on him becoming instantly absent. But the Indians were generalists: a white man had sold them bad goods and a white man or his clan would pay to make it right. At first they came into the settlement threatening and angry, making a fuss without weapons, demanding payment for the fraud. They brought the barrel with them and pointed to the false bottom, the river water they had been sold. The settlers ignored them and went about their business walking around the angry Indians, pretending they weren't there. One Indian man grabbed a passing young white boy and began a charade that the boy would be kept until they had their satisfaction from the white settlement. The Indians were lightly armed with knives, and one settler walked slowly to his tent, shouldered his rifle and from fifty yards killed the Indian holding the young boy. The boy fled, and the Indians were soon surrounded and outgunned and driven from the camp. Someone had the idea to burn the offending Indian's body at the edge of the woods as a lesson to the savages. The next day an entire white family-- man, wife, and two male children—who had camped on the edge of the settlement were found in their tent with their throats slit.

And so it began, the man said. It turned out the white men were generalists too. All Indians passing through came under attack on the presumption that all Indians had been responsible for the outrage. All whites leaving the camp heading west were attacked in some way depending on the size and armaments of the party. Small groups fared the worst. All Indians moved away from the settlement. All whites became the offending shooter. All Indians became the offending hostage takers.

Then came a man who identified himself as Joshua Able this time.

They said he shifted from one foot to the other almost like he was dancing but standing still, the man reported. Some said he was tall and others said he wasn't so tall, maybe regular size. So he showed up in the camp and listened to everyone about the Indian problem and how it started, the burning, the ambushes. And he thought for a long time, shifting like that from one foot to the other like he was the pistons in a steam engine. Then he stopped suddenly and said he'd like to help, but that people would have to do what he said. He said he knew what would stop the Indian nonsense and put things right. He wanted to meet with the men. My brother-in-law was headed to the California gold fields and planned to go out with the first group who'd have him from that camp, the story-teller reported. Well, he told me in a letter that this guy Joshua gathered the men away from the women and gave them a talk. Mostly the men were shocked by what he proposed. A couple of the men walked away, and Joshua kept talking to the rest. He said they had to think like the Indians think, and that would help at every turn. It was, he said, as if all the rules of civilization, how we treated each other, what we owed each other, how we expected to be treated—these had to be renegotiated in the face of our situation. He said he knew this from experience with the Indians, that he had lived with Mandans and came to know how they thought about not only white people but about the other Indians too. Every group considered themselves the people, and others were people but not *the* people, and that made all the difference.

The sun had dropped behind the trees, hung in the branches pasted behind the leafless trees, and a cold wind entered camp, up from the river. Joshua stood stock still finally and laid out the rest of his plan of systematic slaughter, more like hunting the Indians as if they had to lay

them up in larders like so many deer carcasses, salt them
down, cut them up and pack them in brine barrels. He
spoke quietly under the cold wind but clear as the air,
distinct as the new moon. He said they had to agree to be
butchers and engage in mayhem wherever they could until
the Indians feared them as angry gods who could have their
way with them whenever it pleased, whenever they
displeased, and they wouldn't know what pleased or
displeased. They had to fear; that was the key.

"They have to fear us every waking moment and dream
about us," Joshua said. "They believe their dreams are as
real as we believe the morning sun is real, the coldness of
water. They must know us in their fear. That is how they
will come to giving in and fleeing. We must enter their
history, even the way they tell it, the story of who they are
in the world of animals. We must be God, the angry God
of the Old Testament. We must make it clear to all the
Indians that the end has come for their order of things.
The new order has arrived."

Joshua took the men near him by the shoulders, though
he looked out over the heads of the grim assembly. The
sun was cold behind the trees.

"There will come a time of asking yourselves, of
witnessing to yourselves, about what you do and will do in
the name of this enterprise. The bloodletting. You must
find the place to say yes to yourself, yes to having the land
of the West, of wringing it from the hold of these enemies.
God has given us the land by his plentitude and grace.

God has looked upon us and upon them and favored our way."

The men were looking at their feet then. My brother-in-law was among them, he said and he wondered what sort of people they would become if they followed Joshua. He said it was hard to turn away from Joshua's words. They seemed to hypnotize like a mesmerist

The slaughter began on a Saturday when five men including Joshua went out to engage any Indian they could find. They followed the river upstream until they saw small smoke and then ambushed a family camped on the riverbank. They shot them and then under Joshua's direction slaughtered the two males, one female and two children like cattle and hung the pieces in trees to attract crows and fish hawks and raccoons and wolverines—the meat eaters. A leg with the haunch attached was hung over the river from a branch of a cottonwood tree and fish came to the surface to slurp at the trailing blood and fragments of meat where the men had sawed the flesh ragged.
The next group out had the advantage of the story the first group told about coming to witness for the necessary slaughter.

My brother-in-law wrote that he was in the second group, and the shy Billy Shoan began to tell what had happened in the first group and what the blood ran like into the water and how the children curled up like worms when they were shot. The children were hard to unbend when it came to the task of butchery.

The man stopped talking and looked off into the distance.

Then they went out, five of them and Joshua like a king leading his army out from a city. But these men were not as steely as the first group. *He* was not as steely and sure. They rode out one day from the settlement, and the landscape seemed completely without people of any color. The river below where they rode was the color of lead, of dead things, and the light was so thin in the late afternoon they couldn't tell where it was coming from, the sky or the land.

The two men at the table got up to leave, one shaking his head as if he didn't believe a word. The second man returned with a fresh beer for the storyteller and sat himself down again to listen.

The story teller continued. So this Joshua rode ahead poking his eyes into the bushes and sniffing the wind like an animal as if he was a cougar and the Indians rabbits. Joshua's hair was shaggy and stuck out of his hat in fistfuls, stiff and black as any beast, and the men coming behind said they could smell sulfur roundabout them as they rode slowly. They found another small camp of Indians and killed them all from the cover of trees. They burned all the belongings in a pile and again slaughtered the bodies and hung them in trees.

The man paused. I didn't know what to believe, but in Germany we heard stories that there was no rule of law— for good or bad—in America. The Americans pretended to construct laws and then the wealthy used the laws to enslave the poor. We thought this arrangement sounded very similar to our experiences in Germany and so thought it must be different in America, must be something different that we couldn't imagine and the stories just propaganda planted by the Prussian King and his brothers to keep us at home.

I decided I didn't believe the Joshua story but that it was a morality tale, like the stories collected by the brothers Grimm or the tales of E.T.A. Hoffmann. More like Hoffmann. I didn't know what the moral of the story was, but I kept Joshua in mind as I moved farther West. I heard one more Joshua tale—right between the doctor and the butcher.

A man named Joshua had appeared in town asking questions about the local preacher, according to the tale-teller on a Ohio River boat where I had booked a berth to save my neck from the local stage

The town was farther west. The teller was smoking in the evening on the stern deck of the river boat, the moon had just come over the trees, and my accent had revealed me as a foreigner but apparently not what kind of foreigner. The storyteller smoked and waited for the moon to clear the trees on the far shore. He began talking so slowly that I realized he had slowed down so that I might understand his tale. The women had gone into the dining room to get out of the chill night air. Only men were left smoking and listening.

I must admit there was fraud about in the air, elaborate jokes I couldn't follow about fantastical giants in the north and sailors being eaten by giant fish, I think. The mood was festive; I recognized it from beer halls and gathering of men in Germany. The absence of women gave men license somehow, to become boys again, poking each other, laughing at nothing, trying out new offences and insults. Some were coming and then going, but the group remained about eight or nine sitting on bales and other freight or having dragged chairs from the dining room and then leaning back against the railing on two legs, men congregated and a jug came out. I thought of the liquor distilled in the Alps from some flowers, fire of the landscape. The spirits were touched by the moonlight— burned with another story of Joshua.

The teller's head seemed to sit on layers of clothing collected from different nations and traditions. He might have been fat, might simply have been hidden in the material, but his face kept exuding smoke and from the smoke words, most of which I knew. To encourage him to speed up I nodded and smiled knowingly, and he sped up as he entered his story, felt around in the words for what must come next. I remember thinking the words might be hot as they smoked from his mouth into the river world. Joshua again.

"The local preacher claimed he was a Methodist," the man began, "and established himself in town on that basis. His wife had died of typhus the first year into the territory, died of typhus and of the winter, he claimed, the winter that asked her as a sacrifice for doing God's work. He had preached of sacrifice the Sunday after they buried her, invoked Daniel in the lion's den, Abraham's covenant with God for the blood of his son, Absalom and Ishmael and Jonah and Ruth. Sacrifice again, the next Sunday. The elders asked him to move on to other themes—of redemption or God's ultimate wisdom. The preacher became morose and uncooperative, but people came on Sunday because his was the only church in town, and the frontier town had invested all its spiritual wealth in him.

"The front of the church was painted white but the sides left in raw planks because the lead paint was too expensive and would be until the railroad got closer. The paint came in barrels of surprising weight, so the town sent a wagon for one barrel. It covered the front and the inside and then ran out. From the road, the settlers could imagine the New England village they had left to seek free land. With a church in place they all felt less fragile, less tentative and subject to the western winds. The church, even with its one-note minister, was an anchor. They could get on with the business of marrying and burying as long as the power of God came surging down the steeple into the land. Reverend Altand could be replaced in time; for now he could conduct the ceremony and protect the surety of creed as necessary.

"Joshua, the story goes, came to town in a fine wagon with a pair horses every man in town coveted. He must have come a hundred miles but showed not signs of the travail of the road much less of any travail life itself might have accorded him. He looked fresh as a wisecrack, a local wag announced. He looked like he needed nothing in the world, another observed. And in this West, everyone looked like he needed something—a good meal, some horse doctoring, God's eternal love."

The moon had climbed and grown thorough in the sky. The boat slowed to sound for a curve and came close enough to shore so the men could hear night creatures splash to safety as the engine disturbed the bank.

"Joshua came to town just as Reverend Altand became more disturbed and insistent about the idea of sacrifice required by God in this western land recently wrested from the savages, how God needed more than church attendance from them to buy his indulgence and their passage through the wilderness."

I found myself thinking of how I was throwing myself into this western land, *Geworfenheit*, I thought, my sense of having been thrown by some unseen hand into the West along with numberless others searching the landscape for signs that it had been given to me, that I was earning it by my single-mindedness and bravery. And at the same time, maybe it was a chill up from the river water, I was aware that I could never really deserve the land and its newness, its biblical and uncursed innocence from before the Fall. Both were strong and simultaneous.

The storyteller stopped to re-light his pipe, found it out of tobacco and dug out the ashes with a nail, tapped it on the rail, refilled and fired up again. "So, I heard that this Joshua came to town and unbidden challenged Reverend Altand to public debate on the theme of God's plan for human beings. And it went something like this.

"The town was on the edge of becoming—becoming a place to attract a railroad spur, becoming a place women felt comfortable and proud to walk the streets, becoming an attractive investment for eastern money. The spring mud in the main street after the thaw had been managed by a committee that began life perspicaciously electing the owner of the only sawmill as its chairman. He was, for the honor, to cut the planks for a plank road. The town would find the trees and bring them to him.

"Reverend Altand's unceasing sermonizing on sacrifice, then on blood sacrifice, began to fly regularly in the face of all the becoming, all the promise the town felt it had already earned by holding out against winter, and harnessing summer for crops and trade. Altand grew bitter.

"Joshua, it seemed, simply appeared on the landscape and took enough time to engage the town spirit and then rise up like the biblical Joshua to task the enemy. The debate was part of the entertainment at the summer picnic celebrating the founding of the town, its plat, its post office The land was flat and rose like glory into the hills outside town. Already wagon roads had appeared in each direction with two to the north where there was more water.

"Joshua said he was scouting for the railroad, said he was looking over the lay of the land, searching the soul of the people. God's plan, he claimed, was clear to him as if God had knocked on his head to see if he was home and then commenced to speak directly into his ear in a loud voice. He claimed direct clarity and received knowledge.

He claimed primacy and purpose and could drive doubt
and doubters out of the land God had provided. He
alluded to the fact that the preacher had become distraught
at his wife's death and unfortunately left behind his calling
under the burden of despair. The public forum would
draw out the truth like a poultice would poison."

~ The pipe smoked mightily as if stoked from below in
the night by furnaces unseen. The bank had disappeared,
and the boat ran slowly up a stripe of moonlight that paved
the middle of the river. The mate called out the soundings.
Something large rolled just under the water off the
starboard side in the shallows of a sandbar. All the unseen
parts of the world conspired to make themselves apparent.

"So Joshua"—the pipe sparked again as the smoker and
teller blew out the last syllable of Joshua—"so Joshua made
his way into the inner circles of the town faithful, and the
preacher ranted on the edge and the picnic day came
around hot and blue-skied. Dogs rooted as a pack in the
street garbage and crows sat the fence rails behind the
livery as if assembling early for the show."

(I remember thinking that approximately here in the
story the edges seem all rounded off on the truth—the
crows, the dogs, the garbage, the heat of the day. All these
appeared concocted in the night on the river, and the pipe
stoked in the darkness at even the mention of Joshua. The
tales of E.T.A. Hoffmann entered my mind again out of
the night, tales to accommodate the unknown world: will
there be a devil's elixir, someone who turns into a serpent,
a mysterious chemist?).

"The preacher waved his arms around and spoke of father Abraham's sacrifice. He was following a short patriotic speech in which a politician trying to gain a foothold in territorial politics told the assembled citizens that they and their votes were the plow and furrow and the seed of the new country opening up to the West. By the time Altand had taken the podium, the audience was glowing in the warmth of populist sentimentality and more than a little moonshine and homebrew being passed around. And his church-worn admonitions fell lugubrious and like a wet blanket over the listeners. Some looked as if they had tasted something sour, but Altand glared over their unworthy heads and asked for blood, for first-borns, for forty years in the desert, for mortification of the flesh and essential creed. They bucked like a bee-stung horse. A drunk threw a small root vegetable just missing the hapless preacher's head. A four-piece brass band began warming up for their performance later and began to draw the crowd away. The preacher ranted on as if he hadn't seen or ducked or heard a thing, finally reaching *exemplum* in his sermon, his hands cork-screwing up to heaven."

The riverboat slowed nearly to a stall in the current, seeming to hang between the moon and the black woods. The storyteller re-lit. I shifted so that I could see a certain young woman—oh that young woman--better through the openings to the dining room. She moved so beautifully, spare of gesture, but finally elegant in the lamp-lit interior. She stopped what she was doing (what was she doing?) and

addressed someone I couldn't see. Over the sound of the
wheel in the water I couldn't find her words.

"Reverend Altand proceeded from the soapbox he
thought was a pulpit until he found a place to the rear of
the gathered and then slid himself down the trunk of a big
plane tree and sat.

The reports, he said, varied about what Joshua said that
day. The pipe glowed against the sky just to the right of
the moon. The female beauty of the world passed by the
open window just briefly. I stacked up the night against the
story, against the yearning, against the newness of this
American adventure. Bad-Wurttemberg seemed another
planet, another star.

"Joshua came to the podium and began to speak about
water, how the future of the town was in its water supply,
how its children would be drinking the clean water if the
town dedicated itself to leaving clean water to its progeny.

Joshua spoke: 'And the water can be a balm on the land
or a soreness.' The storyteller worked up to stentorian
tones of biblical apocalypse. 'Or the water can smite both
the high and low with equal vigor. We drink the milk of
the earth and apply ourselves to working land in the name
of our very lives. We have been promised the land by God
if we will fructify and grow plentiful in the land. But I have
seen the lord of chaos lurking upstream as a dead horse
bloated with impurities and putrification, and like a soul
dipped in Satan's vileness. We are at the mercy of our
worst instincts and deadly sloth. We would defecate in our
own parlors by fouling our rivers upstream from where we

drink. Your preacher has said we must sacrifice and sacrifice again in the name of earning God's blessing in this western vale of tears. But the preacher has given to God what is ours to concoct in His name—our lives. I come from the East with news about water—not blood sacrifice but pure wetness of everyday water. Many great thinkers now believe that what lives in water may be of great harm to us. Not just the dead horse, but the jakes, the vile-smelling back-water rotting in the sun, the crapulence of our very waste—in short it is ourselves and not God's wish for sacrifice that can carry us away into the desert. The preacher is a man who has lost his good mind because of a great loss. His wife's life was not a gift to God, a price paid to inhabit this land in His name. It was—like all typhoid— a sacrifice on the altar of ignorance. What we don't know kills our loved ones. Not an angry God but an ignorant community. I offer you science. He offers you his anger and febrile mind searching for revenge on the world.'

"At this Joshua pointed with the force of a thrown spear at the preacher who rose in the shadow of the tree. The preacher proclaimed in almost a squeak the one word: Blasphemer!"

'Blasphemer? rejoined Joshua. 'It is you who claim to speak for an all-powerful God with your mind fractured by your grief. You who presume to bring God to the good people here, but you bring him dressed in the rags of your poor understanding that was shattered by your loss. It is you who make God's great grace a thing of petty and ignorant and pitiful abomination to mankind. You speak out of your wretchedness and claim it as the mind of God. Speak preacher. Speak more to me of blasphemy. Come up here and speak what you say is the mind of God and let these good people choose.' And with this he beckoned the preacher to him at first with one hand, and then with both in a swimming motion as if to draw the man to him by reducing the air between them. The preacher rose seeming caught in the gesture but recoiled and slunk away behind the great tree."

The riverboat tooted at the lantern that appeared on the starboard shore ahead and the lantern began to wave in the night. The moonlight revealed a small landing stacked with bales of something, and as the boat drew closer, several men moved among the bushes to make ropes ready for a landing. The assembled story listeners were caught between the tale and the attraction of watching the landing by moonlight. I saw her moving again in the lantern light, this time looking directly out at us assembled on deck. I came to know her as Mrs. Els, married to the earnest and shy John Els of Muncie, Indiana where his family store specialized in dry goods—yard goods and even plowshares and fence wire. Our boat came to hold in the current just off shore—story, boat and Mrs. Els all stalled in the currents waiting.

The story teller tapped his pipe on the railing until the last of his fire floated off into the dark water. The man sitting in front of me stretched his arms and shifted on a bale. The smell of him funneled up to me on the still air— sweat and excrement, the sourness of food gone bad, and the odor of some elemental error. I thought of *korperflege*, the German culture of maintaining one's one body— brushing teeth, bathing, combing. How on this boat and this way to the West the idea of *korperflege* seemed abstract to me and not even an inkling to many of the men and some of the women I encountered. I remembered my first smells of the West, how I thought I had fallen among animals at first, then how I came to love the smell of Americans and America, the wildness I wanted so much, what I left home to look for. The storyteller also stretched and responded to a question about what happened then to the preacher and Joshua.

"The preacher, it seemed, had already been recalled by the American Board that had sent him forth upon the troubled waters of the West. He had received a letter recalling him more than a month before the picnic but hadn't responded. It took his replacement nearly two more months to reach the settlement, and he was carrying a letter that clearly relieved Altand of his duty. But the day of the picnic was the actual day of reckoning. By the time the replacement confronted him with the power of the Board to recall him, the preacher was a broken man.

"Joshua, the story goes, would not let the preacher's leaving the picnic be the ending of the matter. Joshua kept the speaker's podium and began to catechize the crowd on what they knew of the man, his credentials, his motives, his sanity, his connection to God Almighty. 'What,' he asked, 'was the manifestation that this is a man of God and not a satanic force among us? What mark does he have upon him that he is come to tell you the word of the Lord? The death of his wife was an accident of bad water, bad luck, not a sign that you need greater sacrifice. This is a man the community must care for until he is replaced, but who also must have no sway in your lives. Better the land lay godless than that it be ruled by madness.' And so he ranted on, they say, assassinating the character and life-work of the hapless preacher. He asked the town to temper its pity with a strong dose of reason, the reason it would take to live on the land and eventually claim it in God's name."

The story wrapped finally around a moral for the riverboat denizens—that in the frontier West nothing was as it seemed in the East—that often roles were reversed from the surface meaning of the eastern world. Sane men became insane in a place that challenged the very idea of sanity every day: the insanity of buffalo thick as fleas on the prairie, of fires that seemed to burn forever, trees that dwarfed a man until he felt small inside himself and insignificant in the largeness of the place. The storyteller's fire was out. Andrea Els I would come to love more than my next breath. The moon skipped into the woods on the far side of the river.

I had the rest of the trip to ponder the anti-climactic story of this particular Joshua. The other Joshuas seemed just as likely as this one. Why the same name coming across the rumors, through the tales exaggerated or not? This was not the last Joshua I would encounter in the

American West. I waited for my chance to borrow a bible to re-read the Joshua story to see if I could find there the reason.

I thought the water would become clearer and clearer as we went toward the West. I was wrong. Wrong in two ways: first, the rivers flowing from west to east were brown and turbid. In Germany we learned to use different grades of sand to clear turbidity from water, and once it was clear, we assumed it was good for making beer. Second, everything I had assumed about the West soon proved wrong. The good guys were the bad guys, the bad good. I held my breath across the land amazed and estranged from myself and what I saw at every turn of boat or wagon. I came expecting the rationality of Descartes, the nobility of humans left alone by wicked kings and governments, and instead I found the irrational and magic old world of E.T.A. Hoffmann. I found all the enterprise of Hoffmann's tales: double personalities and double realities, young love with its tragic consequences, the confusion of fantasies and realities, people who could turn into animals and serpents and did, the Devil's elixir. All these and more. So the Joshua tales even without any classical ending or moral rang in my ears as our boat huffed its way out the Ohio and into the Missouri River for the trip north. In fact, the whole West became a landscape of Hoffman tales, sort of a New World stage for Old World plays. I was wrong in this assumption. I was wrong about lots of things.

The boat arrived at the beginning of the Missouri River several days later. We had entered the big water of the

Mississippi and turned north. You could hear the paddle wheel dig in and work the water furiously, suddenly now running against our travel instead of for it. At our first stop, the elegant Mrs. Els, unknowingly bearing my young lust, my heart, got off with her husband and, I found out later, set out for a buying spree in St. Louis to set up their mercantile in Portland, thinking they would travel with their goods across the mountains and into the Northwest. I missed her immediately and thoroughly with the longing only a young man could feel, a young German brewer full of the lusting after all that was new—including Mrs. Els. The Missouri River turned out to be very different from the Ohio, or the grand and flat Mississippi. These three river names had the power of magic spells in my homeland. Young men in Germany said them out loud to each other just to hear them aired, hear them break open the wood smoke haze that hung over our villages. How the West rushed into our imaginations just in the act of saying these potent words like a chant to invoke the passionate gods of all that was not bounded by our towns and our puny experience. The names of these rivers meant sharpened knives and scalpings. Weather bigger and grander than anything western Germany had yet concocted. And bears and wolves and the fabled moose for which we had no equivalent. The first moose specimen sent to Paris in the 1820s was thought to have been a joke perpetrated by incorrigible American naturalists having their fun.

All the way up river I remember thinking how the muddy water would be difficult to brew with. The crew caught fish so easily that it seemed the river was packed with big fish with little space between them for the muddy water, and if the water cleared for a minute we would see the great backs of fish in every direction and the boat churning up river over their green humps. Fish like the herds of buffalo I'd encountered in the stories of the Germans who had gone to America and come back. So very few were the returnees that in Wurttemberg we always assumed that those who came back had failed somehow to really encounter America. The stories went that these who slunk back were the weak people who got off the ships in New York, maybe traveled out to Philadelphia, then turned around and fled back to the old world flying the flag of proven cowardice. Parents assumed that when the boys went out they would not be back unless they became fabulously rich and returned to gather up their parents and to choose among the best of the German girls for a wife. The river is thick with fish. The river is elbow by elbow fashioning a westward course, and too soon we are stopped in this water travel and begin our dusty land attack on the hugeness of the West.

My impression of crossing the land is one of exhausted tedium interspersed with moments of stunning, unimagined beauty—usually off in the distance. For three days we traveled toward one piece of the Rocky Mountains, and each day by noon the mountains seemed to have receded farther than they were at the start of the day. In the fourth day the blue distance between us yielded something toward late afternoon, something of the distance so that the peaks seemed to rise up out of the ground, stand on their tip-toes.

I traveled unencumbered by anything but a young man's patent encumbrances: lust (Mrs. Els never left my mind or loins; I yearned), ambition (I had turned my back on my homeland, family and even history itself and each day felt the great joy of increasing distance between me and all of them. I felt warm adventure on my face and cold evisceration of memory at my back), and hunger. I ate whatever was offered in our wagon train, but there never seemed to be enough things made out of flour. I ate the biscuits as if they were Swabisch dumplings floating on heavy chicken stock. More often they were flat, unleavened but for salt, and floating on venison fat. The brilliance of my first sight of buffalo faded at eating them day after day. But from fort to fort the crossing was accomplished and the water cleared as we went up and through the passes to the Rockies then muddied again down the other side.

Finally, along with Mrs. Els leading the way like Dante's Beatrice and beer always at the back of my brain, I encountered at Fort Hall some version of the Joshua I had been hearing about for several months. I thought at the time that there was no question the encounter was one form of the stories of Joshua. I wondered which one: the healer and mender man of medicine, the butcher of Indians, the voice of civic pride and humanist? Were these all the same Joshua? Which one did I find at Fort Hall?

What form of *Sturm und Drang* affected my very seeing of
this Joshua. Now older, I think I might have seen only *A*
Joshua, not *The* Joshua. I might have entered the story and
found it impossible to see the story without myself in it, so
integral did I become. But enough metaphysics. Here's
what Fort Hall brought.

The unfortunate Fort Hall—its story one of greed and
failed capital and the British discouraging the settlers—had
all the charms of any swamp. We got there in 1856, and I
expected more Joshuas and wasn't disappointed. This
Joshua was a chameleon, a wizard, a warrior, a prophet, and
a charlatan all at once. The form he took when I saw him
at Fort Hall was a man with a wound and the beginning of
septicemia and raging infection. He was fevered and
speaking fevered words thinking they might be his last. He
ran out the words like life lines for himself seeming to hold
on to his heart beat as long as he could make words. He
meant nothing and tried to mean nothing. Just words
tumbled from his face in a sweaty panic. I watched him for
a while, listened but found no particular thing he could
have meant. For me the listening was like when I first
began to understand English and found a word here, a
word there out of the air but no meaning. So I concocted
meaning, usually far from the actual meaning but by habit
of extrapolation, I thought I was understanding.

Joshua—his last name they told me was Will—spoke to
the universe at large, and the sweat flew from him. They
said he would die, but he didn't. It was the water trying to
kill him they said. I found out later that many people had

had bad water experiences at Fort Hall and all along the
Oregon Trail. More deaths from bad water than from any
other reason. And Joshua bellowed and raved, and I could
hear the cold and the hot of his ravings against the icy
mountains and the hot seeping of his wound.

I walked outside the fort in the evening thinking of
bears, not American bears but German bears. When I was
young it was bears I was threatened with, all children were
threatened with; all the wolves had been killed. A bear
would come in the night and eat my hands if I persisted in
my incivility. A bear would know which little boy deserved
to live with his parents and eat good food and which
should be taken into the woods to live on sticks and be
covered in his own filth. In the night there was no hiding
wrong-doing boys and no danger for the upright. I
remember looking at my hands and wondering what I
would do if my hands were eaten off, how I would miss
them for dressing myself and doing school work and
touching the dog.

I walked outside of Fort Hall and Joshua's voice had
become a far-away singing of the lonely sadness that
surrounded the unfortunate place. There were no German
bears here doing the bidding of our parents and the
burghers with their hats and stiff gaits and disapproval of
loud children. I imagined the bears in the West, though I
had only seen them in the distance, as bears that would eat
parents and their scolding, would eat my father but not my
mother. Would not eat you if you laughed, but would eat
you if you furled a brow and reproached a child. These

new bears could smell *pflichte*, all the duty we owed society to maintain ourselves properly. It would make them hungrier. Joshua moaned to the night. The cold stars slammed right down on each side, right down to the black earth waiting for stars. I thought that one thing I could always do here in the West would be to walk away from the fort or train of wagons, walk straight away into the black or even the haze of day, walk away by myself and see what happened. No one would know. I would walk into hills and water and American bears and day by day become thinner and thinner until I became transparent and become the grass itself right in mid step. Joshua fought the battle of Jericho.

Chapter Seven

Fort Hall

It was before Fort Hall, before and then during the long walk to the fort we could see in the distance, that *pflicht* occurred to me. In German this is the idea of getting the right thing done, keeping your tools sharp and ready, cleaning up after yourself, building the habits of good citizen and worker--duty. If you stood in any German village you could see *pflicht* at work. And approaching Fort Hall, *pflight* was nowhere, not even remotely suggested. The fort was cleared out of the forest, a temporary clearing temporarily breaching the insistent disorder everywhere. I thought that maybe it was *pflicht* I had come to escape, all Germans were trying to escape.

My father insisted, his brown mustache twitching like some small mammal captured there under his nose, that *pflicht* was what made us human and what would keep us human. It was what—I could see his eyebrows rise, his finger in the air—children had to learn so that they could take their place in the world, and, more important, so that children could take the place of their parents and continue a society of respect and civility. He would then wax more German: the countryside that rose up on the hills around Lindenbronn had a geometry of fields that spoke of 900 years of tillage; the town's water source and square were established at nearly the same time and bore the imprint of people doing, for the most part, what was right and befitted a race dedicated to serious work and dutiful worship. We—his sons who had recently violated some tenet of this 900-year legacy of decency, and through whose wanton disregard of all duties German threatened to bring low, working in consort, the republic itself—alas, we were powerful forces for chaos in our unrepentant disregard for *pflicht.* At least that's how I remembered my father's speech as Fort Hall first came into view with the chaos of the West barely held at bay. The sense was that whatever accommodations were being made here in the wilderness, they were temporary and provisional.

My father then took me and my brother, miscreants that we were, into his workshop. The fine scent of wood there being worked out of the chaos of planks into the order of bedsteads and bureaus and chairs.

"The tools," he indicated. "I want you boys to look at the tools. I use them every day." The chisels marching up in size hanging from pegs like soldiers marshaled for war, the awls and punches and draw knives and block planes, drifts and saws and turning mechanisms for spindles—all clean and in order, all were waiting to become metaphor before our young eyes, to turn into lesson and precept and homily. "Consider the chisels how they gleam," was my father's version of the lilies of the field from the gospel according to Matthew. Consider how the sawdust is swept up and discarded, the spindle lathe driven by an oiled leather belt, the glue and fasteners, consider how the

sunlight comes into the orderly workroom and makes work
worship...

Fort Hall. My father. Joshua. I suffered from the first
of many dislocations and dream-like states that the New
World hurled at me like apparitions. Once upon a time in
the West I accepted a taste of opium from Chinese railroad
workers who were medicating themselves against the
creosote burns on their shoulders from carrying ties in the
sun. There was the presence of my father in this landscape
still seeking diligence and 900 years of sacrifice and duty.
And I realized how I bore with me the old order and
insistent logic of my German childhood, bore with me into
this American West where forces and creatures and ideas
were abroad that would consume a man like the fever
raging in Joshua.

For example, the people I travelled with took pains to
tell me how God's providence would bring the rains in the
needed season for any crop planted out on the prairie. The
plow would break open the land and out would flow some
essence of earth that would inform God that rain would be
needed in the following months, that His servants were
now occupying the new land and His servants would be
pleading for both his blessing of rain and his attentions to
every fallen sparrow. When I first heard this new science I
thought it was reasonable that I hadn't heard it before since
the Old World had long ago broken open all the virgin land
and attracted God's good rain. And while the metaphysics
of the proposition smacked of Protestant theology—caring
and attentive New Testament God of love—my informer

was so earnest in his belief that surely even the earnestness alone was sufficient to crack open the clouds and bring rain.

Fort Hall was surrounded by tentative and halting attempts at gardens that succeeded only in attracting every grazing creature to their beans and squash including the Indians that grazed the land in seemingly perfect amiability and expected the land to nourish them whether tame or wild, and further that it was their right and privilege as citizens of the earth to harvest what lay in their path. And so the gardens grew by day and fell prey by night to the natural cycle of things in general. A deer grazing in the gardens ended up hanging in the smoking shed from its heel strings. Indians, while not edible by local custom, could be shot at as they passed by at the base of the hill much as you could shoot into the crows descending into your corn rows. One man who I was told had been staying at the fort for a month and seemed to have no farther destination in the West had captured a small, black bear and kept it on a leash like a dog. Each day he said he planned to wrestle with it until it grew accustomed to the bouts and then would grow up to be his fortune when he took it to San Francisco and wrestled it full-grown in public. "Wouldn't that be something?" he asked those assembled. "Who here wouldn't pay to see a man wrestle a full-sized bear that might just bite his head off for you?" And most thought that would indeed be something to see. We stayed at Fort Hall to rest the oxen and stock. I wondered whether Mrs. Els might not round the bend

from the East and walk her lovely way toward the fort. I
wondered if her husband might not have been eliminated
by a single bout of the typhoid or an Indian raid or …
Alas, I thought I might comfort the widow and she might
take to a hearty German immigrant headed where she was
headed before the unfortunate…and she might seek his
protection and guidance and value his knowledge and
training as a brew master, then she might throw in with him
and…

The nights we waited were especially long. On the trail
we all slept at sundown the sleep of exhaustion and a good
day's work. At the fort the trivial task of driving the stock
to pasture and back to fatten them for the final part of the
journey was the work of older children while the men and
women restored their bones.

Joshua, who should have died raving toward the
heavens, didn't. And after a week of returning from his
fever-adventure, he began to walk, then wander the
encampment accepting gifts of food in the name of his
spiritual journey by way of septicemia. We were glad to
feed him though he seemed to have trouble talking now
that the fever had passed. Some thought he had lived but
come out damaged goods. Others thought he might no
longer be entirely of this world and eventually seek out the
shelter of a cave and live out his life there like one of the
Catholic saints. When he did talk he talked like a child. He
shuffled and snuffed the air like a dog nodding his head
while he did it. There was no authority left in the man.
One woman pumped him about his people, where he came

from, and he answered with biblical nonsense. "I walked in godless ways. I come from abomination. I was legion," and so forth until the woman gave up. One day he was gone.

Then nearly a year after I had been in Portland, some men were talking in a bar about a white man who appeared with Indian raiding parties covered in mud. One survivor hid in the woods when his small party was caught alone against a river bank, and the raiding party killed all the men and the mud-covered man began cutting up the dead and was stopped by the rest of the Indians who hauled him away. The survivor reported seeing the slaughterer's face. It had deep set dead blue eyes, he noticed. Eyes like a bird's eye, he said. Or a frog's. The survivor was hiding in the grass behind a tree watching the man hack at his friend's limbs, and the mud man stopped and looked directly at him and paused at his bloody work. The eyes seemed to bore in to his hiding place, to see through grass and tree. Then the chopping and sawing at the limb continued, and the butcher was restrained.

I remember thinking this could have been Joshua or some piecing together of all the Joshuas from all the stories I heard while crossing the country. And it came to rest, I thought, in a beery hall in Portland. But it wasn't the end of Joshua, of the Joshuas. That had to wait until I became something of a first citizen of Portland town, a burgher not dreamed of by my father in Lindenbronn.

Chapter Eight

Mrs. Els

My love story, the story of my love, is one largely of
yearning. Mrs Els, Andrea Els (she pronounced it else),
appeared to me through the haze of pipe smoke on the
paddle wheeler making its way up the Missouri. Then she's
in the window surrounded by yellow lantern light. And
then she's absent, having taken with her husband another
trail west.

It was the absence that filled my thoughts with her face,
her body imagined fully out of long nights awake with my
lust, my imagined trips with my mouth over her body, each
lick and nuzzle making her more passionate for me until
she becomes driven by my touch to touch me back—there
and there and there. She became Lilith and the West itself
as I lay drenched in stars and my own heavy breathing, the
two inseparable. Mrs. Els. Andrea else. Somewhere else.
She became in her absence large enough to fill the horizon.
A hawk cry. A voice from the water. A young German
man's longing had no barriers: I took such liberties with the
body of Mrs. Els, her orifices, her hair, her complicit and
passionate nature that our love fed on the previous night's
licentiousness to find more invention, biblical lust. Alas,
Mrs. Els, Salome, the whore of Babylon, Bathsheba, Ruth
in the alien corn—none present, but all were accounted for.

I was unapologetic each night as I ached for her. And she came to me naked after I tired of removing her clothing piece by piece. Finally she began to beg me to do things with her, to her, limited only by what I imagined she whispered urgently into my ear. Hurry dear Henry. I want and want.

When I next actually saw her, however, she was spattered with the gray clay of Oregon City's main road. Her husband looked pale and unsteady rolling a barrel— pickles, I imagined, maybe whisky. Heavy, in either case. Making his heart pump ungodly strong and wild in his chest as he hit the mud with it. He slipped and kneed at the barrel to keep it rolling, but finally the barrel just pulled him upright, and they both stood there in the mud. She tried to help him break the barrel back again so he could roll it, but the clay mud suction insisted the barrel rest right where it was. I waited and watched Mrs. Els strain at the barrel, her sleeves rolled, I thought provocatively rolled, the flesh glowing against her husband's yellow-dull skin. She looked stronger from their journey west, her muscles filled with the dark silken nights, the lashing rain, the treacherous river fords. He looked drained by the same, emptied of human color. I watched until I could not watch more, and then I wordlessly entered the barrel battle and heaved it up onto its rim and passed it back to Mr. Els on balance. Again he rolled it a short distance toward the waiting wagon and lost the balance again. He draped himself over the barrel breathing heavily.

"With your permission?" I asked and took over the barrel.

"My husband has been feeling sick since we got here," Mrs. Els said. "We appreciate your help."

I rolled the barrel through the mud and onto a plank walk then up the loading dock and into their wagon. When I came back down she offered to pay me to load the rest of their store provisions, and they would pay me in flour or whatever I needed. I refused the payment, but took the opportunity to enter the Els family as a benefactor, a friend. I was feeling exceedingly young and strong, and I could sense that I was emanating tendrils toward Mrs. Els that vine-like wrapped her ankles, her legs, her thighs, her waist, her breasts. And Mr. Els stood by breathing heavily, his head hanging, his bowels in full typhoid revolt. He scurried off toward the jakes behind the single-story building that guarded the loading area.

Mrs. Els thanked me for my help. Then she said hesitatingly, *danke shoen*, and looked at me for approval. I smiled. So she was educated and beautiful. How long before her husband died? I remember thinking unashamedly.

The West was very hard on some dispositions. Some of those who returned to Germany came back to the village wan and pale as if they had been to the New World and seen ghosts, peered through the veil and came back altered and chastened. One young man of a shoemaker's family, the fifth of five sons, the son for who there would be no shoemaking neither in our village nor the next villages outside, decided he would go to America where he heard good shoemakers would be paid a premium, especially in the West. He reported that the difficulty of the journey across America had been unimaginably long, longer than from Lindenbronn to Moscow or farther still, to the ends of the earth. To China! He said it seemed a lifetime to him putting one foot in front of the other each day, falling asleep in the crushing darkness and then waking to follow the wagon's tongue—the tongue set out facing the dying sun each night to mark the new day's direction—in endless repetition of the day before. He said he began with bad bowels and longing for his mother's cooking, that each day of game tasted wilder and uncured until he could hold nothing down. He was nearly dead when he reached the coast, and his family sacrificed dearly to get him a boat ticket home. He came home tiny as if he'd been eaten from the inside by the worms of that huge space. He was three years regrowing his vigor, and parents pointed to his example as proof that America was not for the frail of constitution. I had hoped that Mr. Els might gently, gently succumb to westness and vastness and wetness in Oregon. I might have pushed him into the Willamette River that day with a feather, scooped up his wife and made off to some castle with her. Just south of where we rolled the Els' barrels, it was rumored French Canadian trappers had a community of multiple Indian wives and were living out some stockcaded version of licentious life only dreamed of by European royalty, of some Louis the XIV sexual intrigues. Except these trappers had no castle for me to

flee to with my captured Mrs. Els. Except their lair of
iniquity would be as muddy as the dockside clay, as soaked
as Mr. Els' cheap boots. Maybe he would catch his death
on top of the fevered yellow skin and diarrhea. I was a
young man seeking beauty in the death of my fellow man.
I wanted and yeaned after the beauty of Mrs. Els and the
vastness of the new country. I had the kind of constitution
the shoemaker's fifth son lacked. Oh, yes, he died in his
village after recovering from America completely. Two
years later, my mother wrote me, he died while working for
the blacksmith; a horse kicked him squarely in the face.

Mrs. Els tended her husband while I brokered my
passage down river to Portland. The hem of her dress had
collected a rim of gray mud by swishing over the landing
ooze, and now when she moved she hurled the weighted
circle from side to side as she tried to help her husband
maintain his footing. I returned ticket in hand as lustfully
strong as her pitiful husband was weak. I wished him
illness again, wished to comfort his grieving widow, wished
to set her up as the mistress of my brewing empire. I
suggested to her that she brew some hops-water for the
comfort of her husband. That she find a place for him to
rest (to end his days chanted my lust, ashes to ashes).
The affair of murder in the West was a business of
variation on a theme. Bodies were discovered like the
bodies of animals in the streets. But there were murders
allowable apparently rooted in what the victim was
wearing—a victim in base clothing, the rags of the woods,
and the murder was not always taken seriously. Should the

victim be well dressed—the mark of a citizen—the
authorities took the situation very seriously and pursued the
murderer with all the civic force they could muster. Had I
decided, had my blood decided, to murder Mr. Els and
make off with his wife, I might have been pursued up and
down the rivers of the Northwest from both banks. Mr.
Els retained the clothing of his class in the Midwest—the
store-keeper's shirt and sleeves, the vest of his class like a
badge of engagement, and though Mr. Els' clothing had
suffered from the travails of crossing the country, the tight
knit of his wool, the high collar, shirt studs would have
qualified him as a citizen. And any region bent on seducing
new citizens into the new land would have to wring out the
landscape looking for murderers and thieves who preyed
on its most precious possessions—the folk.

I watched Mr. Els, pale and slightly yellowish, bent over
and walking in pain back from the Jakes.

Mrs. Els would not suffer widowhood long in this
country. There are the men who come into the Northwest
with families and the men who arrive alone seeking any
work. The men who come to the West alone are always
looking for an unattached woman, and lacking the church-
going versions, they will pay for an evening with a woman
of less virtue but more, if rented, enthusiasm for sex. Mrs.
Els would last in this marketplace only until the dirt settled
in Mr. Els' grave. The West has short mournings, fast
pregnancies, and so quick old, as we say in German. She
belonged to his class, and her badge was an apron. When
he dies of his paleness, his leaking out of all orifices, he will

leave his empty shopkeeper's apron, and she may spend a short time as a boarding house cook or domestic for one of the better families, but she will soon have herself a new husband and a plumpness under her apron. But before she falls into her second marriage, I will be there and make Mrs. Els my own.

Ownership in the West. I read the Englishman Locke, I have watched the puzzled Indians trying to figure out what the papers waved in their faces have to do with whether they can cross a meadow and hunt there, and I know the lust for things—to own things.

In Lindenbronn, families own things together. We had a clock, dishes and utensils, an ice box, knives, and our house. My father had his tools and tool shop, and none of these belonged to the family. The king had the grazing land, and we paid rent to graze two cows. I had a small knife and my clothing as a child. When I left for America as a young man, I had my small knife and clothing in a paste-board suitcase. The suitcase failed quickly, and I had a bundle.

As I looked at Mrs. Els and the sallow Mr. Els I found myself wanting more things, more stores, my own silverware and plates and shelves of provisions and small figurines. A cuckoo clock. And Mrs. Els in charge of them all. I could feel her hands arranging and re-arranging things until with a smile she was sure of the correct order, her hands on her hips, asking me to move that to a higher shelf, this to the window sill. I willed the death of Mr. Els through accident and disease. And when he lingered sallow

and thin-skinned until his veins showed through, and while
Mrs. Els tended him and also tried to set up a store, and
when the river bank covered itself in blackberries and
shuddered with feeding birds—I waited. The typhoid
somehow abated though it left him a wraith with hollowed
eye sockets and bluish skin. Certainly, I thought and
longed for, Mr. Els will expire in God's own good time,
and I'll be there for the grieving. That Mrs. Els was
perfectly distraught, worked until her hands bled, tended
her husband lovingly was lost on my young-man's longing
for her. I stayed around keeping myself from the Portland
enterprises waiting and waiting. I helped move provisions.
I pretended concern, asked after his health, became a friend
of the family. But Mr. Els awoke each day again, defied the
night, and sucked another breath and then another.

One afternoon she drew me aside to thank me, noting
she couldn't have kept going without me, how much of
family I'd become, how the hard life had sorely tested her
husband. She lay her hand on my arm, and I thought she'd
feel my pulse banging there from her touch. But she
sighed and turned to a broom, clutched it to her and
searched instead for a cleaning opportunity. *Pflicht*, I
thought. She makes so good attention to orderliness and
detail. A lovely woman. I would see her outside the
building they rented: sweeping, hammering, fussing the
frontier wood into tidiness. I would come back from
Portland, and she was there in the shabby store they'd
opened with short provisions. I never saw her husband
working and asked after him.

"He seems tired all the time," she said. "He doesn't seem to get over it like the other ones did. He says something hurts when he moves, something that feels broken. The doctor doesn't know either. He thinks he just needs to rest, and he'll get better. So that's what he does, Henry. He rests."

She pushes hair back from her forehead and tucks it into some kind of hair catcher she had pinned there. She has no idea of my interests, only my attentiveness. I keep up my German-ness between us. I ask again after her husband. She lays her hand on my arm and sighs. She's so young, and I was so young and her husband had grown tired and old and faced the wall curled on the cot in the corner. His steady breathing sounded like work. He rustled the mattress stuffings like a child idly shifting while we talked in the front of the store. I could hear his noises. His shoes sat by the door limp with his absence, and I wondered what would happen if I declared myself to her, took her hand, then held her around the waist until I could draw her in and our skin would touch.

I would spend sometimes three or four days in Portland, and each time I came back up river I stopped first to find Mrs. Els at work, her husband breathing at the wall as if he panted into a miasma there. No one was sure what was wrong with him. He was being treated with a reduction of hops and celery seed and arnica, she told me. She made them up according to a recipe given to her by the local doctor whose route involved Oregon City and ten miles in any direction. I would have to study the local doctors later on when I needed good doctors for my Portland business affairs—the ladies of the evening—and so I came to know that most doctors practiced a kind of herbal cover-up of symptoms. Mr. Els lived without what we called in German, *stolz*, or pride in himself. His wife admitted to having to keep him clean and brush his hair. He sat at the window wincing at the light, the horses and mud and commerce outside as if the West had reached in and yanked out some vital organ, taken some part of him as sacrifice required by displacement. His wife thought he might be homesick for Indiana. She had heard about men and women coming west and then just giving up to the emptiness and losing the will to go on with the business of everyday—the cooking and cleaning and repairing of the worn out, saddle soap on the harnesses, weeds pulled. This endless business of life seemed manageable with neighbors and family around, but some new arrivals found it overwhelming in the new, raw place.

Mrs. Els was always glad to see me, I thought. I would knock on the window of their store and wave through the glass before going in.

I was working on clearing my English of some parts of the German accent I had so thick at first that many people simply looked puzzled at my early attempts to communicate. Looked puzzled and then walked away sometimes muttering Kraut or Swede or Polack. I wanted Mrs. Els to say: "My goodness how fine your English is Henry. I almost can't detect an accent anymore." Instead she said: "It's always pleasant to see you again Henry. I look forward to your news from Portland."

Dust seemed to cover everything. At first she had dusty circles on each breast from leaning across the counter to adjust the meager merchandise. I needed no help imagining her breasts, no target to stare at. Then she brushed them off, turning only slightly away from me and brushing the resistant dust. The next time I saw her she had made an apron to cover her entire front, but it couldn't cover my longing. And the more I longed after her, the more formal I became as if I could hide my lust in my German stiffness.

"Mrs. Els, I'm pleased to see you again. You are looking well. I hope your husband is feeling better. I bring you news from Portland." I could have clicked my boots and saluted. I could have presented her with my orders. I could have ...

"Mrs. Els., may I touch you on the throat, there, just in front of your ear where your pulse is? May I feel your heartbeat with my lips? And nudge your ear lobe with my nose?"

I tried to visit the Els as a family: respectful and customary. I had learned manners where manners were a social contract that allowed the most truculent of neighbors to live for fifty years next door to each other without open conflict. There was a way to act and if each of us observed the good faith observance of propriety, then we had the basic and understood difficulties of life under control. We had energy then for the unexpected and casual disorders of

life. It was the same German covenant that allowed us to
brew superior and stable beer: yeast and heat and cold and
light could be made to obey the same way each batch.
And yet I curl my toes in my boots when I speak to Mrs.
Els. I recall the church iconography of Lindenbronn, the
somber saints' stares, the heavy light from the window.
Christs and blank eyes of the lambs in order to control my
thoughts. She turns and walks away from me indicating
where there will be a shelf installed when they can afford it,
and her body speaks to me through the movements of her
dress. It is only my curled toes and the hazing of the saints
that keeps me from reaching out to stroke her exquisite
bottom.

I promise to come back with more news in a few days.
I am finding the West agrees with me to the same extent
that it seemed to have gutted Mr. Els and others. Maybe it
was the tales of Hoffman and the uncanny that prepared
me more than I thought. What was it that allowed an
industrious young man of disciplined work habits and
robust health to so soon conquer the raggedness of the
West? Others were undisciplined and energetic. I was
disciplined and energetic. The only obstacle I had to
overcome was my German accent, and I never could. But I
brewed better beer than anyone.

I remember I had been absent and about my business
for a long time, maybe two months; it was a Tuesday
afternoon when I returned to Oregon City leaving my
established foothold in Portland for another visit with Mrs.

Els. I came to the storefront catching my breath from the quick walk up from the river front. The window of the store was blank. A piece of faded cloth hung in the window half torn with a faded blue flower print cooked away by the sun. The store was locked and for rent. I asked a neighbor about the Els family. He, like his new cracker barrel, had just arrived a week ago. I went down to the docks and looked for a familiar face, some memory older than a few weeks. It struck me how new and constantly new everything was this far up river. The world had started the day before yesterday.

I thought of Lindenbronn and nine-hundred years worth of memory and the oppressive weight of it I felt as a young man there. Someone had done and said everything. Whatever you thought you were trying someone had cached the results in an old saying or local wisdom. Don't, they said. We tried that already, and it doesn't work. Here it feels like all tryings will be permitted, and if they are useful, then so much the better.

My father once went before the board of burghers in town. He had a scheme to divert water from the hillside spring into a holding pond that then would be redistributed to various parts of town and even into public houses to serve everyone. The eldest burgher, Valker, listened politely and then when my father had finished, Valker asked him: "What makes you think you stand here, now, superior to all the citizens who have come before you? And what allows you the presumption to assume that none of our ancestors could have thought your scheme? Many thought your thought, and the fact that we don't have such a water system now is testament to the fact that it is not a good idea. Now, if you have some special knowledge or information from God, please, Herr Weinhard, tell us of this pact you have that none of us suspected. But if you have no more than your presumption to change things that have worked for hundreds of years, then please be silent and leave. Well? What is your choice?"

The others on the committee kept their eyes on their papers while the elder raked my father with his eyes. I was peering over a railing near the back of the room and saw my father growing smaller in his skin. His clothes seemed to bag and wrinkle and weigh him down. I had never seen him humiliated before. He hung his head and collected his drawings against his vitals and silently left. At home he said nothing until I asked him, and then he said, "They were right. I was thinking too highly of myself. I was putting myself above the others who came before me. And I was thinking like a child who has to be told that he is being too big for his britches. It was wrong of me. You can learn from this, Henry. It is not necessary for you to repeat my mistake. Learn from this. My error was trying to change things just to change them." And then he retreated to his workshop and closed the door behind him.

No one knew where the Els had gone, whether he had died, what she did with herself, whether they both went back to Indiana. They had come into Oregon with all things possible. Maybe all things had happened to them, I thought. I found out that lacking 900 years of tradition, all things were permitted—nothing was ruled out. That was the wildness of the new world: you could brew the newest beer the newest way; or you could be eaten by beasts you couldn't even imagine. It seemed beasts had eaten the Els.

I didn't find out which beasts until the following year.

Andrea Els watched her husband fail, they said, fail in body and mind but in spirit too, they said. I asked what they meant by spirit, and they said that the soul seemed to go out of him, as if he had become an animal, an aging pet in his wife's house. He sat at the window that looked out at the blank boards of the next building, and he stared heavy-lidded at the planks as if looking at a far horizon. After I lost track of the Els, I found her story in pieces and assembled his loss of soul and her change of profession.

John Els spoke seldom as if the effort drained him and sat afterward studying his broad side of a building maybe waiting for a message from God. Andrea began to amass debts.

Debts in a town where you are known and your people are known can be accumulated slowly over time since those owed know someone will bail out the debtor. But in the West, if you had a debt, you needed to collect it immediately or the debtor might move one hundred miles away and effectively disappear forever and leave you stuck. I ended up owning more than one shabby bar in exactly this fashion. The beer bill brought me partial ownership— as collateral against the debt—and finally the owner simply slipped away into the night. I never lost a cent extending credit to a bar owner secured by the bar itself. If there were two owners, that was a different story.

Andrea Els began to take on partners in her retail enterprise very soon after her husband lost his soul. Spaulding's flour mill in Portland extended her the first credit, then the itinerant peddler of yard goods, the sundries wagon and his needles and pickles and other durable goods, then the landlord finally when he found the enterprise in his building now had many partners each with a percent of the business. The Els, it seemed, had no money for the passage home to Indiana to her people, and the snake of debt had come to sleep under the house. The peddler made the first proposition to her. He would halve her debt if she could see her way to coming with him on a warm afternoon on a picnic in the woods, just the two of them. She went thinking he might be lonely, and her company was all he wanted. But his business deal had more significant and personal goals. He held her by both arms on the blanket, his weight on her like debt, like longing, and took her for fifty percent of the debt, the other fifty percent of which she had no means to repay and would have to concede another picnic.

And still she sold yard goods when she could, but there seemed something wrong in her store when the women came in to see what she had. Now there were three general merchandise stores in town and hers felt wrong as if the light coming in the window was insufficient to show the merchandise. And her husband, visible through the curtain in the back, John Els communing with the blankness of the

world—that seemed wrong. And unlucky. The entire
enterprise seemed unlucky, and there were the other stores,
and more coming. Andrea Els found the long morning
hours when no one came in, found them like stones to
tread and burrs stuck in fabric. When customers came in,
she smiled heartily and greeted them nearly bowing to
them, nearly reaching to touch their feet. They suddenly
felt set upon rather than waited on.

She held out the new fabric to catch the window light.
She was too smiley, too chatty: too much friendly and
stood too close. Some aura of damnation filled the store, a
whiff of brimstone that Andrea's soaps couldn't cover.
Someone had seen her in the wagon with the peddler.
Someone had seen her using the back of the buildings to
walk the length of the town rather than using the front
street like decent folk. Someone had heard she was riding a
failing business like riding a stricken horse. Someone
supposed she had taken to the woods more than once.
What was wrong with her husband? What had the Els
done to lose their humanity and their self-respect? Had
they come west to escape some bad business in the East?
Andrea Els' eyes grew, they said, to resemble owl's eyes,
saucers of despair and barely concealed panic. She held up
through the end as if by wild will drawn from forest places
just outside the mud street and single church that kept
howling wilderness at bay.

Assembling her story was like tapping into the fear of
every teller I cajoled into adding to the tale. Whatever they
were most afraid of—the satanic, the wild, the fragile

civility—that's what Mrs. Els' tale drew from them. My German accent besides the negative side of making me seem stupid to these people also gave me the advantage of seeming harmless as a child is harmless and a person who can be told simple things in keeping with simple gifts of comprehension. I acted the Old World simpleton and thickened my accent to a growl, and they had to ask me to repeat my question. And I did. From them came the rest of the story of the Els.

After the store had definitively failed and the landlord took the rest of the stock against unpaid rent, Andrea Els stood in front of the store with her husband standing in the shadow of the overhang as if the light might be too much for him. Their world was reduced to three shabby suitcases tied with twine. She waited for something, I suppose, because they said she sat on a suitcase at the front of her failure and posed as a waiting person, someone thinking something could come along any time and the sap would rise again in the tree of her life. She waited all day and into the evening. Her husband sat then and curled against the building like a dog. Near dark she roused him and began to wheel their piled suitcases on a hand truck she fetched from somewhere behind the building, and she set out walking and wheeling north toward Portland on the dry side of the road, her husband trailing silently like a ghost. They were like ghosts at the end. The stories that had this end all spoke of the ghosts they were, had become.

Chapter Nine

Economics

I collected stories of the Els, and they all disappeared on that road. It was nearly a year later, I had brought more men from Germany to the brewery and my beer had conquered all other beers, when I took over half ownership of a bar that had defaulted on its beer bill. In the rooms above the bar, the owner had been renting out rooms to awful smelling men, sometimes three or four to a bed. There were the inevitable fights, a fire once that blackened one wall before it was put out. I voted my 50% that we should evict the smelly men and invite some women to take up the rooms for whatever business they might like to conduct there as long as that business had no fighting and shooting. At the very least it would smell better, and being up on the second floor, it might even increase the beer sales and profits. My partner saw the wisdom in my proposal, and I assigned him to find likely women who had business sense and manners. After a week he came back from excursions to places where there were women who might fit our plans. One of the women who showed up was Mrs. Els.

She recognized me immediately and greeted me warmly as if this meeting were the most natural occurrence. I

asked after her husband, and she told me he had died, just
got weaker and weaker and then finally died. Died of the
West, I thought. He had the living juice sucked out of him
by the water and wind and the trees. They had all
conspired against him, against his weakness, and then he
died. Mrs. Els, on the other hand, seemed to have left
Indiana far behind though finally she asked me if I knew of
a good doctor—for all the girls, she said, for all of us, don't
you see. I said I would find one. She smiled, and I
remembered seeing her through the window on the
steamboat. She seemed momentarily to be back there in
that yellow lantern light though the window, the sound of
the steam engine, the tobacco smoke. Whatever
adjustments she's had to make to her new profession, she
seemed to have made them with a certain good will as she
discussed with me how the rooms might be improved with
decorations, what the split might be on revenues, what
supervision I could expect from her, which days for
payments and what sleeping accommodations. She clearly
was the designated leader of the women, and the others
consulted her about privilege and work hours. I kept
thinking she might just be the contractor and not a
prostitute herself until she confided in me how she became
a "professional" out of financial necessity before her
husband died, and maybe that had broken him in the end.
She confessed this in the same tone she discussed how
many yards of cloth it would take to treat the windows in
the rooms. Her voice had become a calm center to the

negotiations, a reasonable force in this scattering of morality.

There were prostitutes in the bigger towns than Lindenbronn, of course. Everyone knew where they were and who they were, and it was assumed that men without women would buy their services, and young men might begin their sexual lives there. The ritual was quiet and seldom surfaced in the business of the town. They were sanctioned as necessity—like death or accident, they were inevitable. But in Portland, the girls and the business of girls was much more prominent in daily life. More than half the men in Portland were working the trees, boats and fields and were men alone. The combination of beer and then women, as I've said, was as natural to Portland as rainfall. The number of family men grew slowly and eventually overcame the other faction, but the girls stayed. I thought about buying Mrs. Els for myself, in the name of my lust for her while I came across the country. I could have her when I wanted, I knew. As I saw how she organized the others, took notes and learned their names and skills, I thought I could have her anytime, and I would wait until she made me some good business here. I was thinking that profit might be even better than lying next to my unfortunate Mrs. Els and returning to all my fantasies about the ins and outs of her. She spoke to me with the respect of an employee but called me Henry same as the days before when she turned away from me to brush the dust from her breasts. I would wait until she could help me expand my brewery and then maybe...

"Henry, the ladies and I would like to see a good doctor to make sure we are not a problem in the community. Do you understand, Henry?" She had dressed for these negotiations like any *haus frau*. "I think it would be a good idea, a good policy, to keep the girls clean of unpleasant symptoms. If word got around that disease was here, we'd only get the drunks instead of the regular traffic. We can expand into more rooms eventually when it's necessary, but we will have to build a reputation for being clean ladies."

I told her I had already found Dr. Cruikshank and paid him well to tend to others. I said I would send him around to check with her and set the ladies right.

The next day I couldn't go near my incipient business, my new foreman, Mrs. Els. I walked the mud and plank roads to the brewery and mourned my own youth, so short a time ago, my own youth. I mourned the river lantern-lit Mrs. Els in my head, her too-soon death we could say in German. Everything happened much faster in this new world: money, death, loss of innocence.

Mrs. Els became one of my top money managers, also managing enough for her own cut that I increased shamelessly quickly to try to buy back my own youth a little. And my second business in bawdy houses came none too soon. First the Scottish business money dried up, then the German money (never very plentiful) and finally the English. And when the English money was gone, there was no capital to borrow, no substance to any of the banks, and the only capital for building in this new town was whatever local wealth persisted in the landscape of stumps and mud. My ladies provided me a much more substantial basis than those—even the established families—than those who depended on the daily ebb and flow of money through their banks. Corbett and Spaulding and Failing and even Captain Couch's fortune—all teetered behind the walls of the banks when the European capital withdrew into the withered creases of the continental purses. We in Portland very suddenly stood alone.

I was less alone than some of the others because I had established with my ladies, and then even more with the comforts of whiskey and accommodations, a regular supply of mobile capital for my other enterprises. My fellow businessmen did not fail to notice that I seemed to have liquid capital when theirs had dried up. I knew it was time to find a way in their world, a way around my accent and into the circles where the money flowed in good times. There would be money for railroads and steamships and river boats. For the city projects with guaranteed returns, there might be room for one more investor besides the usual closed circle. I found a large, clean bag and stuffed it full of money and marked it on the outside so it was clearly money. Then I waited for one of the periodical runs on banks that occurred with each rumor of insolvency or war or lost ships.

It was the Corbett and Failing bank this time. A line had formed to withdraw money. The usual procedure at the banks was to instruct the clerks to work as slowly as possible with each patron, engage them in conversations about family, work, anything, but always give them their money eventually. I had heard that Corbett and Failing had become long on debt and short on cash reserves because they made an excellent long term investment in railroads; it couldn't lose. But in the meantime there would be some shortages if too many people wanted their money out at once.

The line ran out the door and down the block. Toward the end of the line there were some of the raggedy people in a fierce assembly that defied the idea of an orderly line. It seemed as if there might be some kind of impatience brewing. Shouts. It had happened before that the line had grown impatient and insistent, and the bank president or some official came out and spoke to the line. That had gone wrong in the case of the '93 run and several armed men shot in the direction of the bank manager. Though there were no serious injuries, bank officials were loath to show themselves afterwards. The teller slow-down method came into general usage.

The wind came up along with the elevated expectations at the end of the line. I held my bag of money against my chest and assumed a humble position at the end of the knot. First one of the raggedies looked at me and then another. When I had a quorum of eyes, I spoke.
"Is this where I line up to put money in the bank?" I said loudly and in my heaviest German accent. "I hear this is da besser, how do you say, the best bank for safe money." I had my audience. Others farther ahead in line looked back, and I raised my voice louder to include them. "I vant to be

sure this is the putting-in line. I have many monies to put in," and I held my bag high.

What silly drama, I thought. What melodrama they required. I kept on repeating and asking and holding up the bag as if I had stumbled into a bad street play, and I was playing the fool just arrived on stage. I took off my hat to bare my head to the wind. The noise of the crowd subsided like a wave drawing back, and I waited for an answer from them, my hat and bag of money announcing my part.

And then it came, at first a whisper as they answered my question to themselves. The louder someone shouted a question to me: You want to put money *in*? "Yes, yes, of course. This is the Corbett bank? I want to put my money in, of course. I don't have a big enough mattress I think for my money now. I want a good bank."

Someone from the bank monitored us from a window above. Pointed at me. Then there were other faces and then more. I held the bag higher.

The line broke up then. Some wandered off, others just stepped out of line and stood there on the planks of the walk. I moved up in the line until there was no more line, and then in the bank I continued my play and boldly left my bag of money with the gentleman to count. There was no line now but audience, no raggedy now but suited gentlemen to take my deposit.

It took nearly a month before I was invited to a meeting of parties interested in Portland transportation investments. I adjusted my accent to include myself in the discussions as thoroughly as possible. I left my deposit in the bank as my contribution to the pool of money going into the bond that would begin Portland's bid for railroad service. I would participate in the profits that would surely follow. If the bank had failed I would have lost my money. But I knew that Corbett had sufficient real estate and merchandise holdings to cover the deposits and would have held on eventually in most of the cases I could predict. So there was little risk on my part, my little theater.

In Germany I remember these public gestures with oversized hand gestures, these public demonstrations of the body politic—these were common. The representative of King Frederick would make himself publicly available and the local landholders would publicly announce their intentions to hold public meetings and vote their concerns and the whole public display was really about maintaining their advisory capacity to the king and his historic habit of listening to them in order to placate them for higher taxation. In Freiburg that was how the people kept rights, by public demonstration and gesture. In America it seemed a useful public display to establish and keep. And I found myself appreciated, maybe not for my acting, but for the public gesture. Henry Corbett said not a word to me about that day. But the invitation came, and I was admitted to the outer ring of the inner circle.

This inner circle had access to the municipal bonds being sold, it seemed, to a select few citizens—old Villard, Dolph, Colby, Hoyt, Lewis and, of course, Failing and Corbett and few others—who could afford the sums associated with civic improvement and the guaranteed rate of return that was variable but most often approached ten percent or more. And then there was the refinancing when interest for certain projects could exceed fifteen percent. Since I was on the outer edge of this circle I could expect the sweet investment guarantees as long as I didn't immediately display my ambition to enter the even sweeter realms of re-finance now covered by the old families and Captain Couch and his son-in-law, Cicero Hunt Lewis. At the first meeting I said very little. The cigar smoke was holy temple smoke blessing everything it touched and then ascending with its benediction to the high heavens. Here was the English, Scottish and some French power. I was the sole German. I cleaned off my accent like I cleaned my shoes, left the muddy out on the street. I tried not to look the principles in the eyes, not to make them feel they owed me anything for my bag of deposit money. The fact that I was in the room was sufficient gratitude, and they knew it. Corbett, Spaulding, Failing, Lord Airlie's representatives, and two San Francisco wholesalers I had never seen before, and the others in the smoke like so many salmon steaks. The topic, in the abstract, was always how to keep the enterprises that generated revenues from faltering or, God forbid, failing. These civic bond sales were considered gold in the banks short of the apocalypse and the second coming of the Lord. The people would need more and better water, more and better roads, more and better everything, and they would be taxed for those needs. The standard for all calculations was the pile of statistics for last year—population, taxes collected, land under development. More of everything this year meant more money for everyone who invested.

The outer ring of the inner circle: I would need a wife to fit my new good fortune. Mrs Els, alas, Mrs. Els would no longer do, though we had already come to an arrangement that she called the "man alone" arrangement. I assumed she had several of these besides me. She always seemed busy organizing the other ladies, setting up the new ones and refining the comportment of the regulars. My hunch was right about having ladies upstairs in clean quarters with an orderly business. I had a cash flow untaxed and steady as the evening breeze off the Willamette River. I made more friends of more bankers with some less dramatic deposits, but kept my old friends too. I was in no hurry to let my recent business associates know my sources of income. I knew they all had pre-tax practices—everyone did—but for two reasons I wanted to keep the new flow of cash private. One, there was very little competition except among lower priced amateurs and these presented a number of tactical problems for men seeking company— disease and robbery being the main two. And, second, the well run professional houses like Liverpool Liz's Senate saloon in the North End (never raided because it was out of sight in north Portland) and Madame Fanshaw's across from the Portland Hotel (southwest and consequently raided occasionally to assuage public consciences) were very public both entering and leaving. And Portland's main families would have nothing to do with these bawdy houses, neither investment nor patronage: dens of iniquity, perverters of the family life. But if they got wind of an investment opportunity as rich and anonymous as my ladies, they would find a way into the cash stream either as a shakedown from the law or a percent of the investment end. I wanted access to the civic trough, not new partners. I had bought out George Bottler as quickly as possible. I rounded up the money from the German community and then repaid that with interest to keep my landsmen on my side. I hired German speakers, the newer they were into the West the better. I had become something of a Count or a Duke to them. They knew the model from the old country—the man with power and land and money who should always be cultivated for mutual benefit. That was why my two workers had nearly beaten to death my public detractor, Bartholomew Cummings. They were eager for my approval, yes, but even more to cultivate a sense of debt in me to ensure their employment and advancement. I was surprised to learn how fast we all fell back on the old country rules when we were lacking any particular rules in the new place. That's why I always tried to hire Germans: so much was already understood in the social contract. And it was why I would find a German wife.

She was presentable, tractable, and almost serene. Her English would improve quickly. She had some sense of the arts and could talk about painting and opera music. After my panting after Mrs. Els, I worked that lustful manner of life out of my system. Passion had its place in a young life

but not in the life of a serious businessman. I decided to
tell Mrs. Els about my plan and my intended.

"She's very young then?" She said, not as a question but
to establish a certainty. "She will give you children. And
you will need a very large house, my dear Henry." She
curtsied next to the bed though she had not a stitch on.

"She will indeed. I will write my parents to tell them
she is German and the wedding will be German and the
food will be German. My father will be sadder than my
mother not to be at the wedding. He loves weddings with
his large Swabisch sentimentality, and he always cried even
if he hardly knew the couple."

"I'm sorry for him." She came back to the bed. "My
wedding was attended by all parties from both sides. All
the portends were excellent. It was summer, the sky clear.
It shows me the way of the world Henry. I could never tell
then that the world was lying to me."

Mrs. Els had found her status in life perfectly acceptable
once she had been reduced to sex for a livelihood. But she
kept a remnant of her old idealism in a special cage of its
own, and occasionally she took it out to publically humiliate
it with reality.

"Henry, will you tell her about your business with us?"

"Will she be a better wife if I do?"

"That depends on what kind of girl she is. Will she
learn your business dealings with the brewery and then help
you succeed even more? Will you talk to her about money
at all? Henry, you have the look of a man who keeps his
own counsel. I think you will ask this girl to be a public

wife to your public life. I think you will come see me again
after a while."

"Mrs Els." She would nearly always flinch a little when I
appalled her with her own name. But not this time. "You
will always be my special western woman."

"I will always be your New Land whore, and, Henry, I
wouldn't have it any other way. You are exactly what the
West needs, a man of many parts, each part lying to the
others." She laughed without a trace of anything but
delight in her own discovery.

She was right. I preferred my literal truth to reside
wholly in the brewing of beer: the temperatures, the
feeding of the yeast. That was the only solid reality I knew
or wanted. I had come to see the thin layers of competing
fraud that made up the rest of life. How hard was that to
figure out? My accent was a layer, my smile for the
Corbetts of my world, their shared largess, the surface of
the river in late evening that appeared as a solid light and a
source of the thousand swallows skimming the air and
water. Layers.

"Henry, I can help you keep this business very quiet if
you will trust me even more to run the ladies and expand
the number of rooms. You wouldn't have to be very close
to any of this. Henry-the-brewer is all the public needs to
know. But you need to give me more of the business to
help me work hard. And also you'll have to buy out the
clumsy bartender. He's of no use to you now. You keep
me as a partner, and you don't need him. You'll just need

to come around now and then and pick up your money and take it to the bank."

Mrs. Els sat in the evening light, a naked woman making her case for a lucrative arrangement of profit sharing. I could see how well the ladies were working out, but she was right. I'd need private screens in place for this private business, and Mrs. Els would be the perfect manager. She seemed to have no problem with my need for a German public wife. She showed no signs of jealousy or covetousness beyond our business deal. She accepted my gifts and affection with the same gracious smile she used when she turned away from me that day in her store to brush the dust from her breasts.

Her nakedness on the bed that evening or any other evening was no burden to her either. She stretched into the warm air like a swan unfolding its wings to try the firmness of the air, and then touched me lightly on the arm.

"Henry, you have never had bad fortune sit on you like an anvil. Maybe you never will. I hope so. All I had left in the world to make myself right with my creditors was this," and she raised her palms to show me her worldly collateral. "Once I put things back and everyone was paid off, then he took so long to die. So long and so slow, like he was holding on to some cliff inside and couldn't let himself fall, though he slipped more each day. At the end he was just empty with the trying, his eyes burned out and blank with exhaustion. I loved him and watched him die. At the end I watched very carefully because his life had become all the lives I saw around me too. Everyone would go through some part of what he was going through. Fast or slow, Henry. Faster or slower we would all empty out and let go. And some part of me knew I was watching the most important part of being alive—the ending of it. And my love could not change one dark pain he was having. I saw he was dying alone, and we all die just as alone, overwhelmed by shadows and our own fear. This became so clear to me. I don't tell anyone this, Henry. Only you, so you know you would be taking a partner who has become a realist, without illusions or animosity about how life is. How life is, that's what I saw in my husband's coming undone by things I couldn't see or even guess at."

She sighed and smiled as if she'd made her case. She pulled the blanket up to cover herself, the effect of which was excusing herself and leaving the room.

I was a young man building what I thought was something the equivalent of founding a dukedom in the new world. I saw myself as inscribing a family crest with brave deeds and heraldic lions to carry my blood into eternity. Mrs. Els' version of life clanged like cast iron when I longed for the ringing of noble alloys announcing my ego to the future. I was too young to appreciate how she had cut to several essential truths in a single sad tale. I imagined she had lost so much so fast—her husband, her self-respect, all her money—that she had come to taste only the bitterness of life. I was growing richer every day, my prospects for great and lasting wealth seemed limited only by my own application of energy, and an American dream first dreamed in a German village was coming true.

Poor Mrs. Els, I thought. She will be the perfect partner because she wants so little now from her hard life. To be young is not necessarily always to be wrong; it is just a lack of complete information that makes it seem that way. Our pairing was in a logical world unholy. But in our world there was a perfect symmetry to the thing because where we met was money. The brewery was becoming more than just the Northwest's finest. My beer was carefully made and so batch after batch was stable—the stable that allowed it to be shipped to Japan and Russia and China. I was making beer as fast as prudence and science would allow. The earlier attempts at brewing by others, amateurs by any German standard, produced fickle and unpredictable slop. I'd had to give away my first barrels to Japan to prove that the beer was good. The Chinese were even more demanding (Germans had already been there). The arrangement I had with Mrs. Els gave me the capital to experiment with my export. I started with Seattle, then Alaska and finally the far East. I heard through a middle man that my beer was being sold in Tacoma by the man beaten by my workers, Bartholomew Cummings. It seems he had prospered in his second attempt at commerce. I silently wished him well. Whoever sold my beer, I assumed, was on my side. I was still so young.

I paid off my temporary partner handsomely and became unscripted partners with Mrs. Els. I don't ever remember calling her Andrea, the name I might have used every day had time and events worked out differently. I think we both embraced the perversity of using her dead husband's name between us, maybe for different reasons. She had found her fate difficult at first, but then she came to embrace it. She said the prostitution was just to pay back all her debts. But while engaging in the business of selling herself, she claims she found a kind of peace after the initial humiliation.

Most of the men needed what she called "complicated kindness" to be able to work and survive in the hard West. The skin, hair and breasts that they bought, was the part she claimed was not particular to her. It was woman. The other part was simple. It involved the male part entering the female part, and that *was* particular to her. That intimacy of those two parts, she said she learned to feel, was simply between those two parts. And she claimed, something like an actress would do, she decorated the skin and hair and breasts as she would apply makeup to go out on stage. She spoke of the entire enterprise in theatrical terms. The rare brute who refused complicated kindness in favor of ravaging, she learned to handle with her own kind of reaction. She said she would "go crazy" when she was attacked that way. She began to cry out incoherently and then mixed in God and Jesus and even learned to vomit on demand, and that ended the attack. The smell, the thrashing and religious babbling seemed to work together to halt the violence immediately. But these were surprisingly rare. Most men wanted what, she claimed, all men wanted, even the violent ones though they didn't know how to accept it—the generalized woman and the specific woman part—nothing more.

Once, she said, she was beaten until she passed out and then raped. But she didn't want to say anything more. She rolled her eyes as if that was sufficient to dismiss the beating. She said she was never afraid after that; the worst had happened.

She sat on her bed, our bed that afternoon, and gave me her perspective on the business. I realized I was still seeing her through the window across the deck of the Missouri River boat, and I would never get any closer. What had happened to Mrs. Els had been something I couldn't really know about except as she gave me the partial stories and eye rolling that would have to be sufficient because it was all I would get. She became the perfect business partner. We had no contract, no legal status whatsoever, no obligation to each other beyond financial benefit. She could have cheated me on the books, but didn't. I could have demanded more of her ladies, but didn't. We kept the perfect marriage of logic and mutual need. When I decided to take a German wife for public consumption, I never considered giving up my arrangement with Mrs. Els. And I didn't. Eventually she ran six houses for me, houses with a bar downstairs and ladies up—all the same. I liked that she found the formula on the first enterprise and then repeated it down to the flowered curtains and feminine bedspreads. Any visitor to one house could feel comfortable in any of the others. She became completely the business manager and took her cut, her percent of the whole. I liked the uniformity of the places. Like the science in my brewery— warm side, cold side, clean tubes and kettles, same temperatures each time—Mrs. Els brought science to our prostitution project.

The project might have tainted and delayed my entrance into the outer ring of the inner circle if each of the principles there hadn't very quickly seen the business value of my venture and become my competitors. I had the distinct advantage of the skills of Mrs. Els. They all—the inner circle—came late to the trade. And there were others like Liverpool Lil who had a head start on all of us. The first families of Portland concocted a species of holding company to run the prostitution in order to keep a sanitized distance between their reputations and this source of income. There was too much money at stake to leave it all to one German immigrant.

Very quickly we were all competing for the good Doctor Cruikshank's medical services.

And there came to be a competition among the proprietors of bawdy houses for the services of the best girls, girls who attracted the right customers, girls who were, like any commodity, worth their price. The pricing structure started out looking like this: Top class girls (young, intelligent, good at conversation as well as the rest of the business, imaginative) would go for top prices of $5 to $20 all night; the next class were not so young, still skilled but at more everyday prices, $2 to $10, and usually for shorter periods of time; and finally there would be the utilitarian girls for the woodsmen, the riverboat men, and these would have a comfort price of under $1 depending on age and comeliness and civility. The cheapest girls were veterans of silver camps and railroad cars and waterfronts on the west coast. They usually began and ended each day drunk, and civility, I'm told, was often negotiable hour by hour. For the best of the girls, 50% of their price went to the house. For the new girls, 80 or even 90% to the house was a sort of initiation fee to be renegotiated by Mrs. Els as soon as a girl established her clientele. None of this, except for the sexual nature of the business, was any different than men working the boats or the woods, or an apprentice carpenter for that matter. Pay rose with the competence of the worker—it was business. You brought in more money, you made more money. After an initial disgust with the whole enterprise, any businessman could see the relation between capital and investment and demand.

Sex and beer, for example, shared a great deal by way of marketing. The important difference between the two became portability. The sex trade was fixed to a place with costs associated with that base. Beer, if well made and stabilized, could be shipped long distances. My excellent beer went from Portland to China, Russia and Japan where it set the standards for purity and quality and then spawned local imitators.

But the girls. Alas, they were more perishable than beer. The damnable syphilis that had come from the fetid East, the gonorrhea that left men walking flat-footed in old age like circus clowns, the boils and welts and sores—these were all part of the fragile nature of expensive and cheap girls alike.

I'm sure each of the girls had a complex and engaging story about why she ended up doing what she was doing. Mrs. Els set the standard here. I assumed in every case that the girls enjoyed the money or they would not have been in the business. By the late nineties there was no question that a woman could work in business in a number of secretarial and support capacities and didn't have to choose the bawdy life, and so we all assumed any girl in the ancient profession was complicit. Mrs. Els made all her managers responsible to her if there was any abuse of the girls. Sex was business and business was sex. An injured girl was a broken barrel. At first we had a number of doctors to see to the girls in all the ways they might require attention.

Syphilis, I'm told, is the scourge of the profession. We had our doctors look over the girls who want to work. Lesions, rashes, swollen lymph nodes, even what the doctor called a telling clumsiness—all these were grounds to fail an applicant they tell me. On the other hand, there is always a certain shortage of the best, best earners, best girls. That particular combination of youth and worldliness Dr. Cruikshank calls prime. We settled finally on one doctor, Dr. C., because he seemed most competent at reducing symptoms and keeping the ladies working.

He looks something like the wild cattle I saw on the way west—long reddish hair and the bright blue eyes that nearly wash out the rest of his face. He seems not to have eyelashes, but on close examination they are fine and blonde and probably keep the dust out though they were not cosmetic. He, besides the red mane, looks nearly hairless and pink like a newborn mouse dressed in wrinkled wool winter and summer. He doesn't sweat. He bills me by the girl, by the head he calls it, like a veterinarian. He also seems to be quite immune to the charms of this particular stock, and that fact keeps him efficient and busy in my employ besides his regular practice. He is a man who eschews the company of the rougher men in the bars, fastidious in his pink way. He has always claimed to me that he would marry someday, but the day has probably passed him by. He keeps the company of the finer families as much as he can. He seems to not hold my German accent against me, and I think that he saw me early on as a man who would be influential in Portland given time, a man who could eventually do something for him or at least set a fine table for him as guest. In the West there were a number of men like Cruikshank who looked for a place to insert themselves into the fabric of a city and then wrapped themselves in the warp and the woof until the end of their days. A new country not only presented these opportunities to men of a necessary profession—doctor, veterinarian, dentist, banker, engineer—but required the Cruikshanks as an antidote to the inherent feral roughness of most men and some of the women.

He came to see me one afternoon in early March after I had set up my second brewery.

"Doctor, some whiskey to chase out the wet?' I asked him, knowing full well the answer.

"I would, thank you." He sat closest to the fire and kept his coat on and buttoned. You'd think a man of inveterate coldness would have chosen a warmer climate, California, for instance. The conversation soon came round to his fees and retainer for regulating the girls. I said I wanted to make sure that my girls were as free from disease as the food on my table at home. Besides it would be good business if men came to realize that my particular stock was clean and certified.

"As has your competition," the doctor said, holding his glass up to the fire to warm the whiskey. I raised my eyebrows, and he continued. "There seem to be a number of...what? Entrepreneurs in town, from the best circles, who believe as you do. Men without women will pay handsomely for companionship, especially clean, certified companionship."

I see him look away into the fire.

"Let's just say the best people. You could name them yourself if you thought about it for a minute." I knew exactly who they were. He held his whiskey glass up to the fire either to enjoy the amber light or to show me how little he had left. "Of course, these men never officially acknowledge prostitution as a part of their financial empires, but the fact is they keep that money building by taking risks with it. And you and I know how profitable the girls are. Low investment and high returns."

"Would you consider, doctor, an exclusive arrangement with me? I'll make it worth your while to tell these other men that you won't treat their girls." I was thinking that if I could have the cleanest girls in town then I would eventually have most of the business in town. I did the same thing with beer: clean water, clean hops and clean kettles, pipes and tubes, brewers' hands, barrels— everything clean made better beer. Beer was food. The girls, in a way, were food too.

The good doctor took his time thinking over my proposition. The other men would find other doctors, I assured him. He said he assumed they would. And had I asked him this same question just a year ago, he might have said yes. But now, well now he had become a recognized expert on treating the girls and their several maladies. He was well paid by all concerned and didn't think that any exclusive deal could make up for the breadth of business he had going for himself. "The best families," he kept saying over and over and shaking his head and smiling. "You'd be surprised who has employed me in this town to take care of their prostitutes." His laugh was nothing that acknowledged funny, nothing quite human. It was more a contented gurgling ending in a croup-like hack and then a catching of his breath. Being in the doctor's presence was almost always disconcerting and left me pondering these western peoples when he was gone.

It became a contest between the families and me to gain the good doctor's services. I put the problem to Mrs. Els, and she promised to see what progress she could make toward gaining the doctor's services exclusively for our enterprises. She reported back about a week later that the doctor was a stubborn case: he wasn't interested in free sex or more money. He seemed to want the solicitous attentions of all the parties vying for his services. He had found two apprentices to work with him to keep a larger and larger number of women symptom free and to work for all parties who would pay him. He was fast becoming Portland's unofficial health service. And while this presented me no particular financial problem, I could predict future problems when the doctor had established a thorough monopoly. He could set any price he wanted, he could consequently negotiate premiums or start-up fees, and he could then, I believed, even take over the houses one by one by simply awarding or withholding his services. At least that's what I would do in his position.

I can now understand that probably Doctor C. had no such ambitions. But then I thought everyone calculated a stronger financial position exactly as I did. That belief served me very well in most cases, first as regarded the beer industry, and then for improving the various financial positions I was allowed by the families and their connections. Everyone of importance seemed to think that way.

I made a mistake concerning the doctor. I failed to see the simplicity of his position, of his wants and needs. I failed to be wise.

Doctor Cruikshank had no particular genius except for his learned skills in treating the symptoms of sexual diseases. He learned, it seemed, to manipulate tinctures of lead-based compounds that the women took orally, and his particular skill was not to sicken his patients in the process. He could shorten their lives in the long run, but could not keep them from working the next evening. I will grant him that skill. Otherwise, he seemed only to really want being needed and courted on a regular basis. I mistook this simple need for incipient greed, alas. To my youthful, should we call it energy rather than hunger for power, to my youthful energy it appeared that the doctor was challenging me on a very personal level. I could not own him, he seemed to be saying, and furthermore, he appeared to be headed toward owning my business, my ladies-business anyway, eventually. I see now that I brought Old World calculation to New World. In this West there was plenty of room for all kinds of entrepreneurship and growth, and every day the possibilities for growth and opportunity grew larger and larger. In the Old World all the economic growth seemed to have stopped in the 15th century when brewing territories and land ownership had solidified around concentrated wealth in the hands of few. It was later that I realized my enterprises in Portland were growing as they might have had I lived 400 years earlier in Germany, and I was acting each day to grab as much wealth as possible while the sun shone. In the Thirty-Years War in the 16th century, men were tortured and killed by forcing them to eat their own shit—the Swedish dinner, they called it. I don't know why. I had no need to resort to these tactics to build my empire.

There was room for everyone, I realized later. For everyone. For doctor Cruikshank and his modest social ambitions, his need for affection. For even misfits like Bartholomew Cummings and his rantings. I can see my treatment of both of these men as follies of my youth but follies with consequences as all follies have.

Doctor Cruikshank became a point of contention between Mrs. Els and me. She believed we should pay his fees and tend to our own business. What a beautifully simple solution she had, I can see in retrospect. But I needed to head off what I considered a dangerous man seeking power. His poor red cheeks, his portly frame, his enthusiastic laugh at nothing that I could find funny, his lip smacking at dinner, his dainty raising of his napkin to wipe away a morsel—I was offended by all of it as I conceived layers of falsity and fraud, illusion being perpetrated to eventually steal the fruits of my industrious ways.

I knew if I asked my cooper and his cohort to deal with Dr. C that I might get the same result I had with Cummings. Could I ask them to temper their punishment? Who then would I get to replace the doctor—his apprentices? Had they enough skill to replace him, then could I own their loyalty to such a degree that they wouldn't work for the others? Could I come to own all the bawdy houses in Portland without offending the other money? Would they publically own their houses in order to protect them? Why couldn't I share?

I can almost laugh now at the shadow of myself pondering these absurd manifestations of greed. My only excuse is that greed and all its incumbent urges drove me every day, drove me across the country picking up English words here and there, learning the ways of this mixture of people and brutes so that I could found my financial empire. It was greed that made no detail too small: the names of harness parts, the terms for various forms of monetary interest alike. My greed was also lust, and they were the same. We were all, it turned out, victims of the West itself.

Chapter Ten

A Partnership

It was tiresome rain with no change morning through evening, a November kind of rain in the second year of my partnership with Mrs. Els. The doctor was doing what he called his monthlies, so he could be free later in the evening for a dinner engagement at the home of one of his patrons. The doctor was growing rich, and I was growing wary of his new power. I had been to a German tailor that afternoon and bought myself several suits made with English cloth, the same kind I had seen on Corbett. I had my tailor make vests too in the colorful German manner so as not to look too close to the English cut of my peers. I suppose I had grown tired of Dr. Cruikshank or Dr. sheepshanks as I had begun to call him in the presence of Mrs. Els. She had again gently taken his part, saying he was doing a good service to the ladies and not asking any more than his wages for it.

"But he is a blob of fat sputtering in the fire," I suggested, looking for any way to depreciate his stock. I sounded like a petulant child even to myself. "He's a pig that walks upright." I was doing no better. "If I could get rid of him, make sure that none of our competitors got him, I would. But if I just dismissed his swinish presence (I was thinking *Swinehund* in German) he would only work for them. Maybe I should have some of my workers run him out of town."

She never took the bait when I confronted my own ego so directly. She thought he might prove more useful to us by simply employing him and paying him. She thought he was a lonely man and only wanted friends and a place in the world. A modest need.

Something about this man, the arrogance of his medical skill, made me want to have him work for me in some menial capacity, cleaning brewery remains, elbow deep in the stink of fermentation waste. That he knew one trick and made that single trick into wealth bothered me, bothered my sense of justice. By all rights this man should never have succeeded in this new world of hunger and greed. His own hunger and greed seemed insufficient to the steaming enterprise around him. But he grew fat, and he grew smug, and I grew more and more outraged. Maybe it was the proportion, the scale of his small gesture in this Portland of large gestures: my standing in line with a bag of money, the Corbetts and Captain Couch and their bets on progress.

"I think, Mrs. Els, that we should not expect long service from him." I thought veiled threat was all I was capable of then. Plus, I found being measured for new clothes made me hungry for Mrs. Els' body for some unreasonable reason of power. I touched her face.

"Will your new wife miss your companionship this evening?" she asked.

"She has headaches. I think she may always have headaches of this kind." I threw my hat on the chair. "But she makes what you call the small talk quite wonderfully. The other wives she makes comfortable. The men at parties want to puff up and impress her with wealth or knowledge. She knows when to be silent. And she has headaches."

"I can see you've worked this out among you Germans. Henry, what is it you Germans seem to have as a covenant between you? Religion doesn't seem to matter: Catholic, Protestant, Jew—you are all Germans first."

"Ha. You should see us in the old country, then you would see we belong to our villages, then our regions…" I realized I was saying "hour" for "our," ladling out the accent like chicken soup. "…and after that we are west or south Germans and then finally we are German." I took my tie off and opened my shirt. "But here we are all Germans first, my dearest Mrs. Els. Surrounded by these howling woods we are desperately Germans first."

Mrs. Els sat on the bed, her knees up and her thighs making me more German by the second, my accent getting comic even to me. She brushed at something invisible on the inside of her thigh.

What a short interval between the person of her journey west and this woman in front of me. She had been very prairie buttoned up—a girl—and then something in that dark visage and her husband's loss of his soul, some Mephisophelean incubus that rose out of the chaos of the woods…well, something burning, anyway, with other fires

142

than the *gemutlichkeit* of civilization. I always know I am carving hard wood when I fall back into the old language. Something...

"...something radiant in your thighs tonight." I was distracted and moved from philosophy to lust by the simple brushing of her thighs. And she saw the effect she was getting and not only continued but slid her hand deeper between her legs.

"Come here Henry. I have something even more radiant for you tonight."

I knew much of her skill at love making was learned in the trade—the skillful ladies always made more money. But I didn't care where she learned what and from whom. When we started, so slow and lubricious, how she used me to touch and prepare herself, how the store keeper's wife needed to rid herself of all clothing and me of mine so we were Adam and Eve, so thrilled and still so slow, until neither of us could stand the slowness any more, and we began to move together and move with all other lovers in the world, everywhere and every time.

Our partnership grew into industry with Mrs. Els the vice president of the combined commerce of about fifty ladies; the number ebbed and flowed with available cash from work on the river and in the woods. If I had been very clever I could have anticipated this cash flow based on civic and industrial projects, amount of wood cut and shipped, and miscellaneous projects. I think I should have been able to place with a certainty the exact number of women we needed based on our percentage of the trade and then calculated to average number of sex acts per day of the week and then balanced by the influx of money based on my inside information and then...

I discussed this precision business-model with Mrs. Els. She laughed and said I needed even more information: the average number of girls who had and would have enough money not to work for a while and needed to shop and maintain themselves, the way the long-time girls synchronized their periods somehow by the moon and living with each other and then... She laughed again and reminded me there was never quite enough information to make an accurate business model for this kind of thing. Maybe beer, she suggested.

Beer *was* more precise and tended to hold still better for the kind of business information I needed. But it was between the two, between the gentle chaos of the ladies and the solid and patent number of barrels of beer, that the problems lay.

Bartholomew Cummings, one-eyed and disfigured Bart, had become wealthy after his brush with German wrath and youthful overenthusiasm. His face had become a remarkable calling card for him, broken and scarred, and he refused to wear an eye patch to save strangers the sight of his one eye-hole sewed shut like a window with the shade drawn. He had begun to wear his hair long and perfumed and oiled it in the style favored by some Indians who found themselves between the white and ancient world of their ancestors. Bart had found business sense after his beating,

business sense like some people found religion. He became
converted to the study of the ways a dollar moved and
shifted in the landscape. He studied for the priesthood of
mammon and was eventually ordained.

His business had grown like a many-headed thing, from
small economies such as the children he paid to collect
waste wood and gather it together to sell back to families
needing hickory and cherry for smokers, to the greater
enterprises of retailing my beer, the very retailing he
seemed incapable of before his beating. What is it that a
man learns from being beaten into unconsciousness, what
does he learn from severe and long lasting pain, and what
correction comes about from memory of such pain?

All very speculative and philosophical, but Bart
Cummings brought all the metaphysics to bear in a world
of action. I heard later that he had put out a call for some
other man of action to come to him and be rewarded after
causing the equivalent pain to me that I caused to him.
This he claimed in the name of biblical justice—the eye for
the eye. And it was said he would point at the very eye he
meant, the eye in the real world that was emblem and
simulacrum of the cosmic justice he sought. Very shortly
after his call for justice, I heard about it.

It doesn't seem far today from Portland to Tacoma,
then it was far: it was the Danzig to the Mediterranean—
worlds apart. When I heard from the teamster who
delivered my beer to my enemy, I thought that I was glad
to have E.T.A. Hoffman in my past so that I could
understand the uncanny wizard, the magical figure flying

off against the fog of petty human understanding. I thought
also of simply having Bart Cummings put away and buried
in the wilderness that seemed to nourish him. But the first
time, when he was beaten, there was no one who cared.
Now he had made himself a burgher of sorts, a man of
stature and consequence in the frontier community and so
a man who could not simply disappear or be beaten (no
matter how beneficial that beating had been).

And then there was silence about the plans of Bart
Cummings. I even entertained the possibility that he might
have been drunk and pontificating in public on the subject
of revenge and shooting off his considerable mouth, and
that might have been responsible for a rumor potent
enough to get all the way south to Portland. And then after
the silence had grown ambiguous and then into a gaping
hole in what I knew, then I heard that Bart had found his
revenger to carry out his eye-to-eye exchange. Still I
entertained that he had made all this known and sent it
wafting my way on demon's breath so that I would live my
life in some kind of protracted fear—the best revenge, one
out of Hoffman. I tried to retrace the threat—teamster to
lumber camp to another teamster to someone else—but no
matter who I sent out, nobody could bring me back any
confirmation or denial. Cummings sat somewhere to my
north with his public threatening like a dragon in its lair,
and I could do nothing of any particular knightliness to slay
him. It was said he had hired a man known only as Joshua.
I already had a compendium of Joshuas to pick from: the
poisoned Joshuas who fell silent at Fort Hall, the stories of

the Indian slaughterer Joshua and the healer Joshua. I had thought the whole collection might be a conflation of name into stories or stories into one name. Something like this happened often enough in the West. Someone named Charlie in San Francisco got confused with a Charlie in Seattle and one who made a name for himself (but not a new name) in Portland. Pretty soon the San Francisco Charlie, if his fame persisted, got known as Frisco Charlie the gambler who you had to watch out for at the poker table. So I thought of the Joshuas and wondered who Cummings was sending.

My wife was not a party to the threat; I didn't think she would know what to do with it. I told Mrs. Els, and she thought I could take the threat one of two ways: an attack on me whether rumor or not and immediately deal with Cummings before anything happened to me, and second, I could ignore the whole thing as the ravings of a wilderness lunatic who could not actually afford to be connected to an attack since he would lose all the citizenship he had worked for. Mrs. Els was such a font of common sense and a star to steer by. Her plunge into the dark world of prostitution had given her a serene cunning and good sense to deal with anything. I, on the other hand, had done nothing but succeed at doing business in the West. But the cost of succeeding was that I could only suspect the layers of deceit and duplicity in the real world not having had actual experience with it. I knew the beast was there. I just had not been bitten yet. My typical day ended, when not visiting Mrs. Els, at the German Foundation for an evening of the newly arrived Beethoven pieces played by a collection of musicians gathered from bawdy houses and from the religious community of Aurora—an unholy alliance, but a satisfactory one.

All the brass was newly made by the members of the colony, Aurora Mills, started by a now dead Prussian ecstatic preacher of some sort, the story went. After his death some of the families stayed in the small town and continued to make brass instruments. And whiskey. And some fine furniture.

It was always warm in the German American Hall, always too warm like the great halls in Germany with a fire too big, too much food and drink—more *gemulichkeit*. At least that was how some of the men and women remembered the old country, and so they built fires too big and made the tables groan with food as a kind of celebration and self-deception. Most of the nostalgia, I found, was a lie concocted out of longing after something that never was. I remembered Germany as expensive butter and eggs, niggardly fires and slavish peasants and their narrow lives. There had been no large generosity of spirit; there had been no room to wriggle up, just to fail downward. My sister married a man said to be ambitious but who became only fat with a bad complexion and fatal habit of drink. When he beat my sister, my father hired two men from the next village to beat him and, as with Cummings, they failed to restrain themselves (or he fought back, they said, and they had to attack him harder) and damaged his brain. This left my sister with a damaged husband who earned no money and still tried to beat her because he was left incapable of having learned his lesson. The best laid plans… Alas. Cummings too had become damaged and more dangerous left alive. Justice remained elusive.

The brass band was loud, and the military music warmed the German and Prussian and Jewish hearts. The Jews' religion became irrelevant in this company. The central fact of their lives was that until recently they had been Germans too. The orchestra had added an accordion and several banjos to the meager violins and cellos who labored to be heard over the brass. The conductor was the brother-in-law of someone who, it was rumored, was also the music director for several bawdy houses and kept that velvet supplied with one musical form of entertainment or another. I saw him as a kindred spirit for the new world loved invention. As my home town hated my father's progressive water schemes, so my new home embraced every innovation and urge to improve the muddy streets and stump-strewn landscape. If it was new, it must be better than we have. Each of the two positions had its drawbacks, but I much preferred Portland's penchant for the new. Constant newness always made the money move around and attracted more.

I sat away from the fire where the oldest congregated. And I could feel the manufactured German-ness as if the harder we tried to bring Germany here into this soggy land, the more likely the soggy land would dry up and become what we dreamed of—an improved Germany, a heavenly version.

The women wore themselves buttoned up and frilly. With Mrs. Els, she and I were both unbuttoned and direct from the flesh. But here the German fashion met the English Victorian and both had something of the West for flavor. It was in the shoes you could see the strain. If a woman's shoes were soft and supple then she came from wealth (and the shoes came from New York or Chicago or London). If the dancing woman displayed something of a limp later in the evening, I noticed her shoes were of local manufacture of stiff leather and poorly tanned hides. I thought to look into the matter of tanning chemistry when the beer was flowing properly from my brewery. A woman with beautiful and soft beige shoes whirled past and set the standard for all the women. She must have come lately into the West and all the women kept her feet in view as they pranced out from under her hemline. My wife pointed out the new shoes to me with the mere raising of her eyebrows. I nodded and pointed to her, and the deal was done. I would pay fifty times the local traffic for her new shoes.

It was important to both my wife and me that we maintain ourselves on the leading edge of fashion. For myself I considered this expensive necessity a form of compensation for my German accent, and though I worked and worked at it (Mrs. Els would sit up naked in bed and laugh at my efforts at the damnable English th until her breasts bobbled with joy) I could not make any progress.

My wife claimed my lack of progress was because I could not sing and that lack of an ear left me without resources to hear and then correct my sound errors. She, on the other hand, took rudimentary English to the mere whisper of an accent in three years. She declared English grammar to be fascinating and a reasonable departure from the German.

The night of the Beethoven was always crowded, but that night was thick with unusual spring warmth into the evening and then heat of the dancing. We sat toward the front where the large financial contributors were grouped together in the most pleasant seating for listening—not too close, just far enough away that the music could blend and coalesce to our ears.

The fire came first.

Near the door somehow a fire had broken out just after the music began. There was no way out of the building going toward the back without going through the musicians on the small stage. The rest of the audience shied away from the sudden fire and threatened to crush us against the stage. The fire was noisy beyond its visible size giving the sense that something behind it was feeding sound and power through it. It was a fire of seeming, like a magician's illusion that fed off the trapped heat of the evening. I didn't hear any gun shot in the crackling, but there was one. The man sitting next to me, Otto Friesen, sat dead in his chair, and just as suddenly as it had appeared the fire dwindled and disappeared without anyone lifting a finger to put it out. The audience made their way out the doors past the last of the glowing sticks that had barely marked the

floor boards. Some of us found Otto and the hole in the
back of his neck just below the collar. His neck bones
must have been severed cleanly since his head swiveled
horribly when we tried to move him to the floor, swiveled
as if only some strings of meat held it to the body. He had
a permanent surprised look arranged on his face as if he
were about to launch into a warning cry to the person
seated just in front of him. Otto, I am now sure, was
supposed to be me. But at the time all the men stood
around perplexed by the fire, the death, the Beethoven, the
early evening's beer. *Dummheit*, I was thinking. I have
fallen into silliness of the deadly kind. It will turn out to
have been a trick, a conjuring complete with stage fire and
fake death. There will be a wizard. There will be a white
rabbit from a hat. This is wrong, I was thinking, all wrong.
The next day we were all asking, the whole German
community was asking, who would kill poor Otto? Was
there an accident so farfetched and bizarre that it could
account for Otto's demise? Was there a hidden Otto, an
Otto within the Otto who had made enemies none of the
rest of us could fathom? Otto who liked his cigars, who
traded in hay, tanned leather, sometimes fish, who always
carried German candy for all the children he met. I once
asked him about the candy—it must have been expensive
always imported from Germany—and he told me he grew
up in the north of Germany and never had enough candy
in his life as a child, always walked the streets craving sweet
anything. He said he gave away candy thinking some child
would be like he was, and some child's day would glow for

a while with the sugar. Otto was a romantic, a fine New World German who loved bacon and sausage and his new country. And he was assassinated in my place.

I wasn't certain about this mistake until I began to hear rumors that someone had become so displeased with me that I was to be killed. At first the rumor came to me from one of my young brewer's assistants who had been drinking beer in a public place and said he overheard part of a conversation that declared me a dead man. I was marked by someone to be killed by someone else, he thought, but he didn't hear it all. He thought I should know. That maybe I'd already known something about this bad business. I thanked him calmly and told him I had made a few enemies and some could even hate me enough to have me killed. It was the price of success. And of owning three buildings. I joked that you could own one or two buildings without being hated. But three buildings…and that was enough to be hated.

I knew it had to be Cummings behind it but the second rumor I heard that it could be some brewer I had driven out of business—there had been a number of them—and he thought I had cheated him somehow. What I had done to all of them had been to apply good science and good sense to a fragile food. Yes food. If you treated beer like preparing good food, you got good beer. If you were careless or lazy or stupid or ignorant, you got bad beer. You didn't have to be all of those, just one, and you got bad beer. Beer would not forgive any of those. I thought of how a horse would know if a driver or rider had no confidence and control. Beer knew.

I went to see Cummings as soon as I could. He had traveled to the East on business and would be gone half a year I was told by the man he left in charge of selling the beer he bought from me. I returned home and let it be known that anyone who found Cummings for me might expect a substantial reward. I let it be known in my kingdom. I put out the word. I didn't believe two things: that Cummings was traveling to the East, and that Cummings himself had taken the shot at me that killed Otto Friesen. I knew if you had money in this raw West that you could always find someone (or someone would find you) who would do whatever you needed.

I bought my wife shoes. I returned to my business partner Mrs. Els. I took her champagne from San Francisco. I took her a silk mantilla of such clean black and red colors that it shimmered with the saturation of the dyes. I liked to take her things that made her smile at me and call me "her Henry." Business partner, Mrs. Els, she was doing well enough that she could buy whatever she wanted for herself. But I wanted her to have the things I would have bought her if our lives and the necessities of western financial affairs had allowed us a life together. Mrs. Els, the song I could not sing in public.

She had built a quiet empire for us—no taxes of a municipal kind. She made a kind of tax payment regularly to a single official of the police. She told me she had been having a number of "tax collectors" and that it was never going to be good business to pay off whoever felt like dipping in our business from the police. And so she found someone in position of influence who would receive one payment regularly and who could make all the other tax collectors go away. She showed me once this amount was established how she had built the cost into the price she charged for the girls, and there was actually no loss of revenue. She handled the doctor, the books, the girls, the rooms. I was nothing more than her financier, her investor.

And her...what? She said she was perfectly happy with our business and personal arrangement, and she wanted no more from me. She was always surprised by my gifts. And delighted. She was always my...I called her my other wife one time, and she laughed, maybe at me, maybe at the other-wife business. But she laughed and patted my arm. I turned to finding Cummings after discussing with Mrs. Els that she could have the business if Cummings' clumsy revenge attempts should accidently be successful. She was to tell no one and simply take over everything.

Chapter Eleven

Lords of Misrule

Cummings was easier to find than I thought he'd be.
The rain had been falling for hours without letup. The
paths were deep mud with patches of plank road near
Yakima where the swales would be impassable. In spots
halves of trees were sunken in mire and at one point the
wagon tracks diverged straight uphill away from the road as
if the driver had been hauled off to the heavens. But the
tracks rejoined a few hundred yards ahead. It took a big
team and an empty wagon to pull straight up the hill, and I
had from the brewery a wagon with a pair of matched
Percherons that could have gone up the hill and then to the
stars breathing steady and bumping each other in amused
companionship in harness.

Their gray backs shedding rain, the wagon fragrant of
beer and the afternoon light stagnant without time moving
at all, I closed in on Cummings in his castle. I had heard
about his personal fort fashioned from cedar logs he had
hauled in from the coast. My drivers had brought me
fantastic tales of the fort and more fantastic rumors of
Cumming's festivities held inside his gates. Apparently
buying my beer and reselling it throughout the interior of

156

the new state of Washington had been profitable for him. He, the stories went, regularly shared his bounty with a group of Indians and itinerant white men.

They would lock themselves inside the walls for days and nights with barrels of whiskey and beer and as many females as possible culled from wandering groups and the countryside. The females, some very young, many repeat performers it was said, were encouraged to wear as little as possible and stay for the pleasure of the assembled men. And then they were paid well after days of revelry and sent away. My drivers heard from townspeople that the participants were almost never members of local families but were men who seemed to come out of the landscape upon some mysterious signal, and then the women followed, drawn by the same inexplicable summons. Maybe they came on a new moon, I theorized. Maybe they just knew, the right people knew and only them, and they assembled like ants on a speck of dropped meat.

I travelled with a pair of men from the brewery. We spoke German and moved on the roads as if we were back in the old country taking stock to market. We talked about sausage, when Portland would get a good cheese maker, how poorly tanned the leather was, how sometimes the need for home ached in us all. We also talked about how none of what we were doing—the work, the brewery, the land one of the men bought—none of these were possible in Germany and how it looked as if the Germany that had finally come together bringing all the separated pieces, this new Germany would soon be at war. One of the men was young enough to be conscripted if he returned, and he had no plans to return and wrote to a brother to get out now and come west. He didn't know if he would.

The gray afternoon grew deeper. I had no good intelligence whether Cummings would be armed in his castle, would be surrounded by his own personal army. Rain started then stopped as we entered the Yakima Valley. I had heard of the fruit trees, but we drove into a blizzard of blowing flower petals that seemed to be endless coming out of the orchards. I felt a benediction, a welcome that I was sure would end with Cummings.

By the time we got to his fortress, I was sure he had been informed of the presence of strangers in his valley. The heavy gate, though, stood open and a boy beckoned us into the courtyard where he took the horses to cool and water. Cummings himself did not show. An old woman asked us to come inside a low shed and eat something, so we ate spiced beef, potatoes and waited.

My Hoffman stories were stirred up like the muddy bottom of a river. The boy, the woman, the castle-like log buildings—I expected the wizard, a dwarf, lightning, some far off bird singing and signs and portents. My companions knew nothing of the stories of Hoffman, so I was left to my own joke, to laugh with myself.

After we had eaten, Cummings appeared, but I couldn't tell it was him. Part of the castle effect was a walkway around the second floor like a covered balcony. I was aware of a man in a large hat walking past across the courtyard, but I couldn't see him well out the small window where we ate. He moved past with his hands behind his back like a monk ambling in prayer in an ancient monastery. Benediction of flowers, prayers, food, care for our horses. This, I confess, was not what I expected coming to confront Cummings.

When he had looked us over sufficiently from his calculated distance, he disappeared. I thought he could have killed me twenty times since I entered his compound. We were sitting and smoking after eating; he entered and stopped just inside the doorway.

"I've been waiting for you, Henry. I am not responsible for what has been happening."

His face was frozen as he talked, the damage from the beating now congealed into a permanent mask. One-eyed. He wore a blanket with arm holes wrapped against himself although the weather had warmed, the rain stopped. He continued. "The boy I sent to you came back. He was turned away I think by your people."

"I didn't…no one told me about a boy."

"I think after the poor man was shot at the concert, your people took measures. Maybe they didn't tell you what measures."

This didn't seem like the raving madman who stood in the street insulting me and my bloodline, defaming my name, slandering my reputation. This didn't seem like the drunk who couldn't keep his books straight, who lost money selling cheap beer to thirsty men. I noticed my companions had retreated to different corners of the room.

"Maybe they know," he said, but they shook their heads. "Here's what happened, Henry. Sit."

Even with the tobacco smoke I could smell the flowering trees. The air was thick, and I felt as if I were eating by just breathing. Cummings' face was not so much deformed as just crooked with one eye open and the other sewn shut, one half his lip immobile and the other half smiling and then dropping again. He reminded me of a mechanical face I had seen at the big market in Wurttemberg, a head ensconced in a velvet rag that you paid to ask questions, and then it would speak and the eyes roll, the lips clack. For a price you would hear your future.

"I came to talk to you about the rumor that you are trying to kill me, and…"

"Wait, Henry. Let me tell you what happened, and then you can ask questions."

"OK. I'll listen."

He moved as he talked restlessly, pacing and then stopping, sometimes turning his back on us as if talking to someone we couldn't see. He talked quickly, seeming to spur himself on by flapping one arm.

"Henry I am at fault, and I'm also not at fault. It was a party, an event we used to call them when I had certain friends in for a long weekend. Someone brought Joshua, and within the first minute of meeting him he asked me what had happened to me, how I came to look this way. Well, we were drinking and, you know, carousing too, and after I told him about how I was beaten, he offered to 'render biblical justice.' He said for a small price he could be prevailed upon—that's how he talked—'I could be prevailed upon to seek justice in your name.'"

Cummings did voices, a deep one for Joshua and then his own. The whole effect was of being in the presence of an actor rehearsing a role, sawing the air, whirling around. He continued.

"And so sometime during the night we struck the bargain, I guess. I didn't remember the next day until a day later he came to me and said he would collect when the deed was accomplished. That's him again, 'when the deed is accomplished.' Then he assured me that the world was a better place each time justice was served, wrongs righted, equal retribution meted out, that kind of language like he'd been a preacher or something. I can tell you from what I remember about that weekend that he was no longer a man of God if he ever was before that. But that's another story. So I guess he was an agent acting for me. I heard about the shooting at the German meeting, the dance or whatever it was. I wondered if he might be involved. But I never asked him to shoot you or kill you. I never did. He only talked about justice. Well, then I decided that harming you, no matter what happened between us in the past, that harming you would only come back to haunt me. And anyway, I should have shut up and taken my medicine when you bought me out, not tried to…well, you know what I did. Henry, you are my meal ticket, my source of wealth. You never sent men to take over my distribution of your beer up here in Washington. You could have. I know how that works everywhere else. So you let me be

and let me run my own little business with your beer—
wholesale, retail, just like in the civilized world. I
appreciate that, Henry. I want to be sure you know.
So I tried to call off Joshua. I got in touch with the men
who brought him to my party. They said he mostly lived
with the Indians, sometimes here, sometimes there. They
would see him around, you know. Then they wouldn't for
a while. Then he'd appear again. They only knew his name
was Joshua, and he talked like that all the time. When he
talked at all. I let the word out that I reconsidered and
didn't want him to do anything. I didn't hear anything
back. And then I did. He sent me a note. I have it here."

He read the note, slowly, in the voice he'd made for
Joshua:
My dear Mr. Cummings,

I received word that you had changed your mind about
the balance of justice in the world, what you seem to think
is your world. But the balance of justice is not limited to
your own injustice. You are not the center of the universe.
If there remains an injustice, whether you deem it worthy
of redress or not, the world remains out of balance.
Justice seeks out its agents. I am one of justice's agents. I
will pursue balance and fructify redress without your
money. When the world is corrupt with sin and the
sanctimonious sinner, a good man may not stand by and
allow us all to sink into the sty of sensuality and self-
indulgence that characterizes the unjust. And so your
wishes have nothing at all to do with my actions. I am a

humble servant of right and will act my mandate from God and serve no man. An eye for an eye.

Joshua

Cummings sighed. "I want you to know, Henry, that I sincerely tried to call him off. I think he may be a madman."

Of course I had been thinking of all the Joshuas and Joshua stories that the West seemed to generate—the Indian killer, the doctor Samaritan, the fevered wanderer at Fort Hall. How many others were there I hadn't heard? And now my own personal Joshua. We'd see if I didn't have the connections to send someone his way and intercept his unbalanced quest for balance.

Cummings finished and wrapped his arms around himself and posed. I thought he posed. Was it all the posing of a nincompoop, the same louse that railed against me in the streets of Portland? I thought his story interesting but not entirely convincing. How easy to delegate the responsibility now to some loose cannon. The afternoon light poured through the window and smeared Cummings with light. Was he clever enough to pull off this fraud? Was all this posturing the way he hoped to deceive me now? I leaned toward the destroying angel version of Joshua if only because I had heard his many-faced story over and over in this new world. This biblical figure, this madman, popping up in the landscape. This special fool. This dangerous fool.

Cummings provided us sleeping quarters in his castle. I interrogated him into the evening trying to find the inconsistencies in his story. It was so full of illogic and inconsistent aspects that it had to be true. But Bart Cummings himself didn't ring true. I thought, on the other hand, that Cummings was selling my beer, I was providing him a livelihood to compensate for the unfortunate excesses of the beating those years ago, and Joshua notwithstanding, the accommodation had worked out with great practicality.

The burr under the saddle turned out to be Joshua's world-saving mission to right the wrongs of the earth—his madness. And if I could believe Cummings, there was not much to be done about it except hope that Joshua would be distracted by other walls, other Jerichos, and forget about a mere German brew master in Portland, Oregon. That he would go back into the forest and succeed at finding meaning in the wildness there.

The next day Cummings made sure we were provisioned for the trip home. He had retreated from the drama and posturing of the evening before. He seemed contrite.

"I can only promise that I will do everything I can to stop Joshua. Henry, you have become very famous in these parts."

It seemed as if I was talking to my mistakes, all gathered into Cummings' face, one-eyed and crooked. The things I did wrong in the New World came from the newness. I didn't know what to do because I had no model, no history within which to locate my deeds. I had to make something up because everyone around me was making everything up.

"Bart, I believe you'll try to do the right thing by me. Where could I find Joshua if I looked myself. Where is he known to live?"

"Like I said, he comes and goes from the Indians, from wherever the Indians come and go. They move around depending on the season."

"But which Indians?"

"He's kind of a doctor or holy man to some of them. He knows doctoring. He helps with the fevers they all get. Some die. The Indians I met think the white man has some kind of medicine that makes them and their children get better while the Indian children die from the fevers. Joshua has a reputation. He makes holes in their skin or something, they say, then the skin gets sick and the people and children don't. Then the skin gets well. I don't know what they're talking about. Look at that sky. It's going to rain again. You might as well stay here until it blows past."

He stood watching the sky for a long time then continued.

"I don't know what the Indians make of him. But I know he's always welcome with them. They think I must have been a great warrior, my face. Your men gave me a kind of power in their world. But I couldn't live with them, moving around all the time. But they talk straight with me and like your beer."

We had more time and decided rain or not to head back south to Portland and maybe run into some Indians who could lead us to Joshua. I thought unsavory the prospect of having Joshua relentlessly after me in the name of some unfathomable religious principle that only he understood. I would rather have a man come after me for money or honor or even pure hatred than to be driven to kill me by words spoken into his ear by a voice only he heard.

We left Cummings and his flowered valley and headed south. We asked the big horses to pull us up into the hills in hopes of encountering an Indian camp. When we did find a small camp, I noticed immediately that most of the Indians had very round heads. We Germans have square heads, and I was immediately impressed by the beautiful roundness of the Indian heads, the stocky body and deep brown and red skin, how even and handsome were the women and men alike. They neither welcomed us nor rejected us. Their camp was on a small river, and it seemed they just arrived and were still setting up camp and scurried to let us know this camp site was taken. I asked after English speakers and everyone only pointed in the direction of the river bank as if somehow there would arise there a translator. Maybe they scurried because the rain Cummings promised was beginning, so we pulled the wagon under a cottonwood tree for shelter.

Finally up from the river bank came a young woman and asked in perfect English if she could help us with something or if we needed food or assistance.

"We will stay here now for a short while," she said, indicating the river bank, the woods and even the other side of the river with the sweep of her hand. I thought she might be telling us that all this she had indicated was to be considered occupied, but that we might visit as long as we liked. She smiled I think because she believed we expected the information to be accompanied by a smile. "You are welcome here," she said. "I am Bounty."

I asked her about Joshua, whether she knew of him. She said she did.

"I know the man. He sometimes stays with us and then leaves again. He is welcome with us."

"And why is that," I asked. "Why is he welcome with you?"

"The same reason you are welcome with us. We all live on the land. We share it. Only some don't share the land. It becomes difficult to live when people want the land for themselves."

The treaties from 1854 and 1855 were well known in Portland, and most Indians were supposed to be confined to reserved land, but in practice they continued as they always had, moving around from time to time. When the salmon came thick into the Columbia, Indians gathered there.

I pursued Joshua. "But Joshua, does he come to stay with you in some season? Does he stay long? Is he...predictable?" I realized I had just asked too much and also nothing at the same time. What the hell did predictable mean to her? To a German it was asking something essential about a person—was he predictable? Where is his home; does he come and go with predictability; are his people nearby; is he a citizen; does he have regular habits; is he a man of property and defense of that property? Is he predictable? Beer must be predictable. A wife must be predictable. Friends and religion and money—the more predictable the better. I kept thinking of Cummings' face, the drama he staged for us, the letter and flourishes and penitence. Poor Otto lying in a heap. Poor all of us with all the Joshuas abroad.

Bounty didn't answer for his predictability. She didn't look quizzical either. She just stared at me waiting until I asked something she might be able to answer. "Do you expect him to come in this season?"

"Joshua comes when he thinks he will be needed. We don't really need him now. There is plenty to eat. The people are having good dreams now."

And that seemed to settle it for her. I asked about his doctoring, when the people were sick. She answered with "by and by": by and by the people would get sick, and by and by Joshua would come to them.

They came to stand around our big Percheron horses when the rain let up. Some wanted to touch the pair to make sure of their horse-ness, I guess. Most wanted just to look, to see the huge iron shoes, the heads as big as a child, the long hair on the pasterns. When they were finished or satisfied they simply walked away and went about the business of camp. Bounty stayed with us as long as we wanted to ask questions, like an assigned guide to the portal of her world. She occasionally spoke to the assembled group, I assume about something we had asked. No one seemed to be adding information about Joshua. One man spun and walked away when she said the name in English.

We camped with them that night and descended the mud road again and headed for home in a slant spring light that seemed to come from the land itself. Moving downhill we looked over top of the horses to land and land and land that was the German dream: slabs and acres and hectares and dominions of land. Empires of land. Everyone could be a noble, landed and ensconced in his own empire. All the way back I thought of the Joshua in the landscape, the small and deadly and wild thing that ate the heart of joy. My joy anyway. Like poor Otto the unfortunate.

When I was a child I believed that when you die you got to know everything, and that was heaven.

Chapter Twelve

Home Rules

Mrs. Els, when I told her about Joshua, observed that somehow what I had told her was incomplete. "Because I don't believe Cummings or the Indians or the letter. I don't even believe the stories you heard—the good and evil Joshua. The West is full of stories people make up to help themselves get through the next day. I know I did. I needed all the tired stories—the story of Job, the song of God's death, the hatefulness of never caring about anything again. I tried them all on like sackcloth and ashes."

I could walk publically with Mrs. Els as long as we stayed well into North Portland, its swampy ponds, its hard working patina of cracked paint and raw wood. Here is where the water supply was at its worst. Here is where my beer was the safe thing to drink, man, woman and child. Before the 1890s by which time the germ theory became impossible to ignore, not a theory any more, the dairies would wash milk cans in creeks downstream from outhouses. Typhoid was rampant, so many deaths. And so much diarrhea and vomiting the doctors treated with concoctions of hops and other herbs. So much money the doctors would lose if not treating these ailments that I think they were very slow to embrace public scrutiny of the water supply. Dr. Cruikshank told me he knew of a number of Portland doctors denying those small germs under the microscope, those fragile beasties that died if you even slightly raised or lowered the temperature, that those critters could be responsible for all that human misery. While Doctor Cruikshank kept his private recipes to hide the symptoms of the yaws, the syphilis, he confided in me that his colleagues were hiding their heads in the sands to avoid confronting typhoid.

Mrs. Els walked with me as far as the near north side of Portland where the neighborhoods of my workers began. It would not have been any problem had my workers seen me with another woman not my wife because no worker in my brewery would have gossiped about me. All of the Germans knew each other; we knew who was loyal and who a sneak.

Mrs Els reported to me that some of the lumber workers who came in to be with the girls had become violent. "Not all of them," she told me. We walked under the first warm moon of spring, her story a brutal contrast to the moon through the new leaves. "Just of few of them, but always the same ones. I'm just afraid they will really hurt some of the women. I don't think they know how rough they are getting. Two of them especially. They seem to compare notes afterwards. Laugh about it. I think if I could discipline the two the others might learn from it."

She was all serious business, but she had my arm and leaned lightly against me. I asked, as sincerely as I could under the circumstances, "How much did they hurt the girls?"

Mrs. Els stopped, the moon stopped, the tree buds seemed to whirl. "They left bruises and bloodied one girl's lip. I'm just afraid it might be just the beginning of this business. I know, I know that some of that goes with the nature of the business, Henry. I know the risk part. But no one has the right to beat up my women or even make them afraid. I think that's what really was going on. The men want to make the women afraid and that makes the sex better for them somehow. I want to use some of the men in your employ, not just street thugs. The thugs then think they can enter into your business once you use them. I've seen that happen. But your men can do the warning part— rough them up like they did to my people maybe—then disappear from the neighborhood and go back to the brewery. These worlds don't have to touch very much." Her argument grew more detailed as she talked about prevention as maintenance, developing a culture of mutual respect and business-like conduct between lonely men and reasonably priced women. How all this life in the West was a great experiment in human conduct. How we needed to make up the right things to do to fit the new situations. All while leaning into my arm while we walked the north Portland paths and watched the moon. She was always able, after the death of her husband and then the months I didn't hear from her while she paid off debts, always able to slice into the illusions that surrounded us. The sex we had together was, she claimed, our mutual pleasure, and she had no claim on my life, and she wanted me to know that. Our business together was once again mutual advantage and also without any strings but finances that made sense to both.

I promised her that I could find two men to "discipline" the bad elements. I would send them over and she would indicate the two who were problems. She would instruct my men on the exact nature of the beating to be applied. I thought my two young enthusiasts, Thomas and Johann, who overdid the Cummings beating might be just the right men, since they had already established an outside limit. We had talked about the excess of that beating when they had finished. I took part of the blame for not being very specific about how much beating was deserved by publicly besmirching my name.

Public beating as lessons in civility had a long and honored tradition in Germany. Of course, this was done elsewhere too, in each country to its own specifications and standards. But the south German version was always done in the name of education. Learning occurred at a very swift pace if the beating was done in the name of the larger courtesy. Being beaten was, in some sense, an invitation to come back into good graces and abide there. There was a compelling and biblical logic to a certain amount of that business. The problems arose when the beatings were administered out of greed, revenge, and stupidity, and in the case of all the Prussian Fredericks great and small, politics and intimidation. Something in me embraced the structure and discipline of well administered beatings. Poor Cummings was an unfortunate case of bad measurement. I sent the men to Mrs. Els. I also sent a man to Cummings' next party to see what he could add to what I already knew about Joshua, maybe even talk to Joshua himself. I was thinking that the Joshua business itself might be resolved if I could meet with him and talk about justice in the world. I would ask if he might be the same Joshua I watched escape death at Fort Hall or if he knew of all the Joshua stories that populated the West with his or someone's exploits. That was a path that I would have liked to have followed. But that's not what happened.

Apparently Mrs. Els gave clear enough instructions about what the beatings were for. My men reported back to me that they had done the favor I asked them and done it to very precise specifications, even given a script and asking the two miscreants how they felt about the mistreatment, if they understood that this unpleasantness was also felt by the women whether they were prostitutes or not, whether they now understood that pain and sex were not to be linked with the women. Thomas and Johann laughed. They said they had to promise they would say exactly what Mrs. Els wrote down. That this was tricky while cornering two lumbermen who weren't interested in sermons. At first it was like yelling at cornered cats. But being knocked down a few times they decided to listen.

My men didn't need to do anything near as severe as what happened with Cummings those years ago.

And my Cummings-reconnaissance man came back from the Yakima festivities with a report a little less satisfying. He reported a four-day orgy of sorts that featured beer and liquor as a base for chasing and sex and general licentiousness. But there had been something going on that he and other first-time participants were not privileged to, some quieter activities directed by Cummings. There were locked doors, several kinds of robes and some animals brought into the compound. Whatever went on was done quietly because he couldn't get close enough to hear anything. Joshua, when my spy asked around, was known to only a few and then more by reputation and rumor than fact. He was never sure if Joshua attended or not.

I began to get very busy with my beer—new buildings, worker organizations, sources for the barrel staves, iron works for the hoops. I had no time for Cummings, his parties, Joshua, his veiled threat. Otto's shooting went unsolved and by police officially accounted as a stray-bullet accident, not unknown in a town like Portland. I returned to the full time enterprise of public appearance, man of business, man of property and substance. Man of two lives, but one reputation. I worked to unite myself with my business contemporaries—in personal comportment, in civic goals, in financial success. My business with Mrs. Els, at first just a sidelight to assure myself of a cash flow in

uncertain economic times like the early 90s, soon became a
significant bankroll for other aspects of my empire.

Mrs. Els was an excellent manager of my interests and
her own. Other prominent Portland financiers followed my
lead. Again the double nature of the Portland male
population—family men and men alone—created a
predictable market for willing and reasonably priced ladies.
Henry Corbett copied my business plan nearly exactly.
Payments of sufficient seriousness and sufficiently high up
in the Police Department always produced dividends. The
payments were a simple business tax. And occasional
crusading mayors created a temporary furor that always
disappeared after proper public tsk-tsking had run its
course. Once we had to move all our operations to second
floors or above in order to make sure no children walked
past a working establishment. We kept girls off the streets
in the areas we controlled; we bought band instruments for
a city band that played in the gazebo Sundays in the park.
We bought hundreds of cords of wood to heat schools
throughout Portland. Our contributions were publicly
unacknowledged but appreciated at high levels of
government. One official theory, a theory of civic
pragmatism informed by the writings of William James,
postulated that decreasing the sexual urges of a certain
segment of a city's population decreased crime and prison
time and so served the public interest. *Phlicht und pfush*, duty
against failure to do it right—Mrs. Els reminded me with a
smile that our business kept pressure from building up and
exploding in Portland.

Mrs. Els had taken up new quarters in part of a building I had bought recently. She now had an entire floor of singular and luxurious velvet from France, settees in the English style, silks by the yard for window coverings, and a bedroom she said she had dreamed about since she was a child in Indiana after she saw a drawing of a princess' bedroom in a picture book. The girl had bloomed in the woman who might have been hardened to flint by her life.

My wife had become the director of the German League's women, and conducted lunches with other groups around the city—the English, Scottish, French and Scandinavians. The wives connected the best banks and real estate holdings in the state. The steamship, river and railroad monopolies were efficiently represented. Museums, universities, the medical school and preservation societies were funded, built and dedicated. My wife stayed very busy between children and the business of cultivating connections for me. She had nearly no accent people said. She spoke like the English wives with just a touch of old Germany in her th. I had peace at home and a growing empire in the prosperous West despite market fluctuations. The forest was pushed back each day from Portland. When I built my first brewery building there were curious bears that would wander into our brewing waste heap and help themselves to rotting mash. Now the streets were lit, the walkways free from mud, and sleeping drunks immediately carted off to the jailhouses.

One of my new workers one day, fresh from Germany, addressed me with a German honorific usually reserved for

royalty in the old country. Without guile, I think, he
conferred upon me a nobility postulated back a thousand
years, extensive lands, special and separate blood in my
veins, and the accolades of God and the earth. I reported
the event to Mrs. Els.

She laughed and asked me what I associated with the
title. I told her. She asked me how that title might mean in
America.

"I think it has no meaning here. I think there is a
sameness here that eats the distinctions between people
and then only money comes to matter."

We sat on chairs in her seraglio, newly appointed with
her new wealth. "And Mrs. Els," I said, "Do you think I
am unfit to be a duke, a king, an emperor?"

"Not only do I think you fit, Henry, but I also see every
other human fit for those titles. I have seen many people
with their clothes off. And every time I thought how much
the same we are undressed, how lumpy and flawed and
pocked. I can't say I've seen naked kings and dukes, but I
know how they'd look." She got up and moved a vase to a
different spot. "There," she pronounced. "There is the
right place."

She sat again and looked at me. "Henry, you are still
marked by the old country in many ways. The Joshua
business, for one thing. He is magical, a wizard or evil troll
in your mind. You have the stories to tell that include
creatures like him. Here we see he is mean and crazy, a bad
combination, but not a rare one in the West. Joshua is
everywhere, behind every cruelty and viciousness. As

common as a dead dog in this city. But you insist on seeking him, trying to understand him. If I were you, I'd find someone to pay to kill him. Buy yourself an assassin like Cummings tried to do. Pay him well and have him do what you are unwilling to do." She rose again and adjusted her room: a pillow removed, a small table set by the window.

"What I am unwilling to do? What do you think I am unwilling to do, my dear Mrs. Els?"

She waited, as if giving me the time to figure out the answer to my own question. I couldn't. I was willing to do what was necessary to succeed. I did.

"Henry you're unwilling to walk the street with me in the light of Portland society. You're unwilling to say publicly the truest things in your life. No, wait. Just wait. I know you for a man of great practical patience. But much of that is to cultivate the proper illusions that will make your successes even greater. How many illusions you have built in order to become the duke, the king of your world? All that is a perfectly reasonable proposition for the here and now. I, on the other hand, lead a life of raw genuineness, and so I decorate my living place with pure fancy. Each day I live in a world of syphilis and girls with nothing left to sell but the holes of their bodies. They live with only a hundred useful words, no books or even bright colors. They live... I sometimes look at them and see the potatoes of my youth--covered in mud. We dug them and left the dirt on to protect them in the root cellar. I hated going to get potatoes for my mother. I carried them in my apron. The faded blue of the sack cloth became mud brown. Joshua to me is that mud. He's not magic or special."

"Then why is there always some kind of Joshua—the bible, the old stories? Always one like him who gives flavors to the pot, the flavors of fear and the uncanny. He reminds us that *everything* we see is a surface, an illusion, a fraud. Any minute the whole illusion could break up and crumble, and we'd stand looking at the real world and hating the rawness of it. We can buy so much illusion to soften that rawness. But Joshua is always right there, just on the other side of the flimsy illusion. He's magic. He's God gone mad, and madness is always a kind of magic. He's true. I don't want that much trueness."

I caught my breath. She was looking at me as if I too needed to be rearranged in her room. And quieter then I said, "I can assure you that ultimately there is nothing that I'm unwilling to do. Finally, I would do anything I thought I needed to do. And that's why I get along so well in the West. I came with very few encumbrances since I came young enough. Only the place itself set limits for me. The older ones I sometimes pity since they come out here so burdened with the way things ought to be, how they believed the world should operate. And then it doesn't work that way. Alas, I can see how disappointing this experiment is for them, why they retreat into German culture, the old sayings, long for foods they can't find, become nostalgic for what was really awful and the actual reason they left the old country. But I'll look into your idea of someone to find and neutralize Joshua. Though I'm still not completely convinced there's only one."

Mrs. Els drew me to her. "Henry, you stand like a giant in this practical world. Maybe Joshua is a demon who changes shapes and is a child of the devil. It's sometimes easier to think of men like Joshua that way. I have a sad view of the Christian church at work in Portland, but I'll give them their stories. Let me just say that I have serviced the clergy as well as the congregation in my day. The only difference between the two is hypocrisy on the part of one of them. The posturing, the great gesture, the speaking in the name of their concocted God who fills their pockets. Ah, Henry, I allow for evil and weakness. I even allow for love."

She returned to her busyness arranging the room. I returned to my public-figure part I played, but I wondered whether I would do anything, anything necessary eventually. I had become so used to having other people make the beer, adjust my social position, bear my children. I extended my hand, made my wishes known and things happened. I had no real reason to dirty my hands with the sordid necessaries of the world. Like a king. Like a duke.

Dr. Cruickshank began to be in great demand. He was invited everywhere, apparently a fine companion at eating and drinking. I thought I could keep his services for our ladies, not exclusively, as he had made clear to me, but certainly on a cash basis. Whatever the going rate, I would pay him a little more but not have him at my table like the others did. They bought him twice. I only bought him once, and maybe that was my mistake. I should have been more thorough.

He came to my office at the brewery. It had become clear that the public health was a risk from the drinking water, and that the little things living in bad water, those fragile and tiny beasties, could kill. Typhoid came from bad water, and bad water was the result of compromised public water supplies. At first, in the 1870s, the medical community refused to publically speak out about the "theory of germs" that came from Germany. So much of the medical business was involved with treating vomiting and diarrhea, so much payment depending on these two pillars of health. Dr. Cruickshank told me his colleagues came in two main types—those who studied somewhere, a university or institute, and those who apprenticed to a practicing doctor and then went off on their own. Since no one was licensing doctors, the good ones became good by continuing to learn. The quacks just did the same thing over and over even if the science had moved on to better ideas and procedures. And even when licensing happened in the East, the West retained its own word-of-mouth approval or disapproval of medical practitioners.

My view was that my beer, a least, was always safe to drink, for man, woman and child. It was safe, and it was food. Water was raw. Beer was cooked.

Portland streets were being lit about the time the scientific light had come about water. You could drive a wagon on plank roads on a winter night and see the white-painted stumps like guardians. The gas lights lit the river and the streets all the way up to my brewery. I liked to think that light and science and money flowed together in Portland; they were liquid and civil.

Dr. Cruickshank asked a civil question, or maybe a question about civility. "Why do you never invite me to your house, Henry?"

I replied that everyone there always spoke German and meals especially were a time we journeyed back to the old ways. My wife with her perfect English still preferred to speak German in the house with the servants—all German—and even the trades people. She liked to keep the house a sanctuary against what she called the wildness of Portland. So you would find all that German uncomfortable or we would find speaking English at meals uncomfortable, doctor. Either way, I told him, uncomfortable. It went unspoken the topics of Mrs. Els and our business arrangement. I didn't need to dodge conversational topics while dining, in any language. The good doctor had moved me down in his schedule and was serving some of the families' houses first. Was it the dinner invitations?

I asked him.

"Oh ja, and also no, no. I just am spreading myself a little thin these days, Henry. I...oh you know, bring a certain skill to my work. And the latest science, of course. I have to keep up, keep abreast of what Europe is doing in these health matters. Arsenic preparations are the latest.

And then the chemistry, the preparations. I'm doing what I can. The best I can."

I brought him a large brandy, and we sat looking out of the bar window towards the street lights. I could tell that the doctor and I had two disagreements to work out. One, I didn't include him in my social life. Two, he didn't think our original arrangement any longer in force. I used to deal with these impasses, with Bottler and Cummings, for example, by simply overwhelming my opponent and getting rid of their resistance. Cruickshank would be another kind of case. He had the skills I wanted to buy. He seemed uninterested in arrangements with any of the women. Mrs. Els had suggested that solution. She said she had used the "free sample method," she called it, with the police in the early days, and it worked well. The doctor had other tastes, it seemed. I tried more money, to buy a kind of priority for our enterprises. But more money, at least at the level I was offering, didn't seem to interest him.

"Henry, I am a man who delights in pleasure. It's my life, my religion, my family. I don't see abstemiousness, self-denial, niggardliness as having any value in life. We live. We die. And in between only pleasure makes sense to me. I like warmth and food and company and, and...*gemutlichkeit*, Henry. You have the great word for it. And I have some other fondnesses. Some very personal." He looked at me with raised eyebrows. "And some, like good brandy, not so secret, I'm afraid."

I told him I needed my ladies taken care of. The business depended on the clean girls and timely examinations. I asked the rhetorical question whether I would need to look for another physician for my ladies or could he keep them current and disease free. He only threw up his hands and shrugged.

"Henry, this town is growing so fast. What I would like is to ensure my future somewhat. My future pleasure, if you please. I would like to be able to invest with the big families and you in the transportation options—steamships, railroads, highway building contracts. But no one will take my money. Now I know you are inside on those deals— limited but still, inside. You could get me some participation, I think? I would be very grateful. I have a little money saved up, and well...I have a feeling that this would be a good time for investing in the future. My future, the future of Portland. You don't have beer stocks for sale, do you? That's another direction I considered. There seems to be no end of your successes in that realm." I laughed and said, "Science." That's what makes good beer. Clean ladies, good beer, I told him. The doctor sighed and asked me to consider those options, ways to include him in the civic future of Portland and of Oregon. He knew I held the brewery as sole proprietor and would never compromise my position there. Not after the fiasco with George Bottler. He also knew that I was let in on the sweet deals of the families, but he wasn't sure exactly why, and it puzzled him. My heavy accent certainly didn't ingratiate me to, for example, the Corbett brothers. How had I done that, wheedled my way into the Villard, Corbett, Failing world?

The brandy had loosened up the good doctor. He became more direct. "Henry, I have...I have thought very long about what I want out of life. Besides financial stability, I want people around. And then, well, I once thought of a family life, my own people around. But I have some irregular habits and tastes, you could say. Yes, tastes that would very quickly make domestic life either a fabric of lies or a thinly veiled set of illusions. And though I have nothing against either, for other people," and here the good doctor raised his considerable eyebrows at me to let me know he appreciated my situation with Mrs. Els, "Other people seem to handle it better than I do. I like the tastes of salt and meat and fresh vegetables well prepared. I have, by the way, recently become very fond of your sauerbraten."

While the doctor made his way toward his point, I marveled at his ability with sweet blackmail. I had always favored the system by which my opponent was backed into a corner from which he had no escape. With the families I had insinuated myself into their financial advantage in such a way as to give them no real choice. I had led the salvation of at least one of their banks; they could only say "welcome Henry." But I had no illusions about complete participation. I had not saved their lives, only some of their money.

The doctor arrived at his point. "And so I don't know what you can do for me Henry, with the steamships and railroad investments, and I realize how you want to protect your goose that lays golden beer-eggs, but I would like you to do me another favor, if you could. Then I could have more time to devote to your other enterprises." He cleared his throat and finished his brandy, holding the last of it to the fire before drinking it. "I understand you have become acquainted with a certain Mr. Cummings of Yakima, and that you availed yourself of his hospitality for at least one night. Is that so?"

I admitted it was, and was about to plead that the trip to Yakima had had a complicated agenda, when Dr. Cruickshank stopped me. "Henry, you remember my saying that I had, well, unusual tastes, or peculiar anyway? Well, I have heard that Cummings has regular masked balls or orgies or something of the sort, some kind of parties that actually would appeal to my tastes. Those tastes that I find impossible to indulge in where I live. Without being too specific about my preferences, I was hoping you might be able to introduce me to Cummings or send me a letter of introduction to him. As a favor to me. I think I might enjoy one of his weekends as a sort of entertainment for my tired soul. A man needs refreshment now and then. What do you think?"

And so Dr, Cruickshank, with my letter of introduction in hand, began the first of, it turned out, many weekends with the Cummings unholy crew of sensual experimenters. I'm sure I had no thorough idea of what exactly the doctor's tastes were. I personally had simple tastes though I had been around enough conversations that had mentioned a number of perversions, or let's say variations on themes, that other humans found pleasurable. Among

the most incredible to my German sense of propriety were
the practices that included dead bodies and some animals.
I saw these as the most abstracted forms of sexuality, and I
confess to some squeamishness and no desire to learn
more. My most immediate result was that the doctor
immediately and thereafter provided yeoman services to my
small industry because my introduction to Cummings had
been successful. And that was what I wanted in the first
place. I never mentioned anything about Joshua.

Chapter Thirteen

Spring

It was spring and then still spring—endless spring into the final days of June. Otto buried, the doctor regularly seeking the sty of the senses, Mrs. Els and I growing richer, Portland with many of the trappings of civilization, and then the wild blood just under the skin seethed to the surface. An occasional bear still found its way to the center of downtown at night. There were parts of Portland, near the edges, where the citizens would put out their garbage at night so bears and coyotes could get rid of it. Lacking an active garbage-eating collection of animals, the citizens near the river simply dumped everything into the river—dead animals, waste of all kinds, the occasional human body. The consensus was that the Willamette River took everything north to the Columbia, then the Columbia to the ocean, and the ocean had an endless appetite for human waste. This was a reasonable proposition since every European city did the same thing.

Mrs. Els and I began a project to clean up the streets around our business enterprise. It began with the persuasion of the two men that kinder conduct was necessary with the ladies. And it included, and I think the lingering spring had something to do with our impulse to clean up, hiring workers injured in the woods or on the docks to clean our streets and paint. There was no end of these men missing hands and arms and feet and legs. They seemed to come from a never ending supply of broken people generated by the fierce work. A substantial sliver left untreated could cost a man a limb. Even after Koch's germ theory gave doctors the reason for infection, there was a significant delay until treatment caught up with theory. Infected water, wounds, diseased sexual organs— these continued well after medicine should have cured the causes. Alcohol, tinctures of iodine, arsenic compounds, Condy's crystals and powders, honey, vinegar, compounds of hops, lye soaps, ah the litany of disinfectants. But still the men came to fill our streets with their limps and empty sleeves.

It was her idea. We could hire them and pay them what she thought their work was worth that day. They would tell her what they had done to improve our streets, and she would pay them. They swept with twig brooms. One managed a cart he filled with discarded trash from a day on our streets. Another, one-armed and enterprising, bought cheap white wash and then hired his own crew to freshen the walls of our district.

Some other neighborhoods followed our lead. Our white wash guy became quite the contractor and soon began to dress in a suit and tie as he moved from place to place directing his civic projects. Mrs. Els became the sub-mayor of our neighborhood and began to take petitions and review plans for housing improvements. The actual mayor of Portland, a great crusader against prostitution and corruption in general, began to send messages to her when he needed blocks of votes and other consensus. And she managed our business with greater and greater skill. There were competitors' jealousies, of course, there were street subterfuges, and there was even some infighting among the women currying favor with her. She had become a political person, a businesswoman, a power broker and a benefactress for the injured and disabled. The more complex her enterprises the more enemies she made, the more friends she could count on.

All this complicated life including the two men she had "disciplined," conspired that spring so that I found her killed in the bed of her newly redecorated rooms. Her throat was slit.

My dear Mrs. Els. My first visions of her on the steamboat with the golden light around her, and then her journey with her husband into some bleak portal to hell, his rocking in pain and her compassion wringing out all the sympathetic juices of her life. Dear Mrs. Els.

I had no right to public mourning. I went to the brewery the next morning like every morning, the good and the reliable German proprietor. I walked my early morning round through both the cool and the warm sides of the brewery, the hops and yeast smells rich and singular and familiar—my financial self in the taste of the air. The bright copper kettles like brooding sculptures, the gangways to the top that seemed to rise up the sides of the kettles and then float out of the room, the sunlight on the far wall, then down the stairs into the cool side, the barrels and clang of hoops, the bungs heaped and bright, sweet tang of spilled beer, the clutter of wagons in the yards, the immense steaming horses washed down and amiable for the day's pulling—all my cunning and invention were made into objects and spaces that surrounded me. And Mrs. Els, her blood run completely out on the velvet pillows of her stage props and fancy.

I had people taking care of the arrangements. I always had people to make arrangements—beer routes, hops supplies, the care and interment of Mrs. Els' body. My family would not know or even suspect. I had no room in my life for the necessary rage.

I walked my brewery each morning for the next days with greater and greater precision and regularity until the men knew to the minute where my inspection wanderings would take me. They nudged each other and pretended to reset their pocket watches. I needed to walk and walk and walk my estate like a farmer inspecting fence rows and finding himself in the posts that set out his territory.

I looked for no sense from it, this walking. On the third day I buried Mrs. Els in far north Portland in consecrated ground, a Thursday, just after two o'clock, and the earth that day that received her, I noticed was deep brown and rich for growing things. The men I hired to dig and carry were from the street projects; I never saw them again.

Very quickly after the burial I had one of the more sensible women workers assume the place of leadership, but my heart was no longer in the enterprise. I allowed the women to buy the business from me little by little. The income was useful.

The police had assumed that her death was simply part of the risks one took in that world—the crazy customer, the drunk, the animal. I knew it couldn't have been any of those: maybe one of the two "disciplined" men, maybe a thief, maybe a jealous rival. It was a week later that during my brewery walk I suddenly knew. She had been killed by Joshua. She was the eye exacted for the eye, the balancing of justice. He hadn't needed to injure my body to redress what he considered the cosmic wrongs. All he needed to do was injure me. And he had.

I thought I could simply go back to my family and the German social clubs, my business and investments. These should have been enough for any man to occupy him until death, to surround himself with some kind of illusion that chaos was abated another day. It's all I required. We had talked about that chaos, Mrs. Els and I, and she pronounced that each day the first job was to keep at bay some of that encroaching disorder. And then you could get on with the details of the day, pursue good things and reasonable propositions. But first...

She had liked to talk about what she called "the big things." With her husband she had never found him interested in "big things" until just near the end of his life. And then he didn't want her to talk. He wanted to say over and over how nothing was anything. She told me he'd lost all energy to even look you in the eye. He spoke to the ground, scuffed the dirt, proclaimed the diminished state of all things, how all things had run their course and the West sucked all life from all things and even colors were not as bright in the West as they were in Indiana, and God had forsaken the West and lay his curse on it in all ways. She spoke of his last days with no remorse, not even a sense of loss. She had watched him "grind up like corn in a mill." She said he became powdered and dry and then blew away with the first breath of wind.

I kept thinking of small conversations we'd had: about her husband, about having come west, about water and birdsong and the ocean when she first saw it. She said the ocean was so giant and empty at first that she felt empty too. But the longer she stayed there watching, the more she felt how…she said she saw "many angels" there. I was never quite sure what that meant. She laughed when she said it as if she wasn't sure herself what lurked in the many angels. She told me how the smell of the Pacific Ocean had been on her mind since the first sniff of it. She…
I kept thinking of the small conversations.

With Mrs. Els in the ground, I knew I would have to find Joshua and find out if indeed she was the sacrifice he felt I had to make in order to preserve justice and order in the world. What twisted and mad running his brain connived to kill her, sacrifice her, to the whole world. I thought I would catch him and sit him down and listen to his shooting of Otto and then his slitting of her delicious throat. I worried whether hearing him tell the stories would infect me with his madness, drag me into his lost mind like the spells rendered in Hoffmann. I worried that I could not wait to hear out his madness but would have to seize his throat and squeeze the life out of his face in her name, then do some unspeakable thing to his body, some abuse, some unnatural act to set things a right. Would I become him? Would I have to become him?

I always thought after the interview with Cummings and then the trip up into the hills to find Joshua that I could find him if I put my mind to it. I assumed I could find him the same way I could come west in a country where I didn't speak the language but could engender a successful brewery with just my wits. I might even find a harmless madman who attended orgies and participated in the *contra naturam* like corpse abuse and ritual Satanism out of poverty of the self.

My father in Germany had a cousin from the next village who slipped every day farther from sanity after the death of his wife. He'd had so much of himself invested in her—maybe call it love—that he died when she died, but he kept walking around. His family and friends tried to help him, but, my father claimed, the "him" part of himself was gone. There was nothing to help, nothing to pick up from where it had fallen. There were only shells and husks, my father claimed, and no nut meat or grain.

In any case, I was convinced that Joshua, the storied Joshua I had possibly met at Fort Hall, was responsible for the death of Mrs. Els. I made plans to find him.

I started with Dr. Cruickshank, plied him with his favorite brandy one night. He had always been fond of

Mrs. Els, and he told me a number of times how
pleasurable it had been for him to be associated with such a
reasonable and competent woman, how she made his job
by keeping his patients on medicinal schedules of
treatment. Many of his customers, he said, stopped
treatment once the lesions of their genitals healed, and that
would leave them contagious and not cured. They had to
follow a prescribed schedule to make sure of the cure.
Mrs. Els understood the urgency of this business and kept
her ladies on medications through the cure.

The doctor had been to an event, he called them events,
at Cummings' compound, and when I asked him whether
he had encountered Joshua, he paused and tugged his
earlobe thoughtfully.

"It may be, Henry, that he goes now by some other
name. There were participants, one in particular, who
demonstrated such an enthusiasm for certain, should we
say idiosyncratic sexual tastes that some of the others took
him aside for a conference."

Again I was loathe to ask the doctor for details, and he
was equally loathe to speak out loud what had been passing
for entertainment on these weekends. He tiptoed around
and finally revealed that many of the celebrants, again his
word, as if the entire unsavory occasion had been some
kind of religious or social event—a picnic, a christening, a
parade—gave false or fanciful names. Everyone assumed
that the identity of everyone besides Cummings was some
kind of disguise. I asked him to describe the man who had
to be restrained without the details of what he had to be

restrained from. His description could have been Joshua, the Joshua I met. It also could have been anyone. But the Fort Hall man raging out of his mind from sepsis came in two versions—the writhing sick man talking to his devils and then the silent, recovered man who wandered off into the woods, seemingly to die.

The doctor said he could now take me with him to the next event, if that would serve my purposes, but he thought I could go any time I wanted since I had been his access with Cummings. I needed to wait until Mrs. Els' death faded for me. I kept waking up in the mornings with groggy intentions to go see her, and then waking up fully I had to take a deep breath and then devise a day without her. I had shown my family nothing, not the day of her death, not the funeral, not the long evenings afterward. She was a shadow now in my world, a singular point of reference about which I could not speak to anyone except the doctor, only remember to myself.

I went about the Joshua business, I suppose, exactly the way I went about building a brewery and then selling beer. I admitted the chance existed that some crazy lumberjack, the two beaten men, some itinerant tinker buying a night with a woman with his last cent, some disaffected employee had killed her. But the overwhelming feeling I encountered after her death was that she was killed by Joshua in order to inflict the maximum revenge on me and have me wandering from day to day reviewing the cosmic justice he had wrought. Biblical, essential, root justice. I had seen crazy; I had lived with crazy. But crazy in the West was so common that people had accepted that the new conditions took a new sanity sometimes—new sanity that was crazy anywhere else.

The mountain men were by and large crazy. The first old ones I encountered in Cincinnati had insanity tempered by old age—the rage and fear and delusions all balled into one ancient glare in a ruin of a body. To a man they were dangerous with knives only if attacked. The bar population of Cincinnati had learned to leave them alone, buy them a drink now and then, and they didn't become good citizens so much as harmless. The stories they told, on the other hand, usually for a drink or two, the stories were about insanity—nights hiding in caves, animal attacks, such thunderous loneliness that the wind and water spoke to them. A small fire, one reported, became a circus he had seen once as a child. He had been for months without uttering a word, without seeing anyone. The fire as he watched became all the acts of the circus—the bear on a log, the acrobats, the trick horse riding, the gypsy fortune teller and all the sideshow oddities. He said he watched for hours and kept feeding sticks into the flames as the price of admission. Finally he had to search the grounds around him, and he got back too late and the fire died and the circus died. He told us he cried and cried until he fell asleep. And then the drinks caught up with him, he put his head gently on the table and fell asleep in front of us. Another kind of crazy was the women. Like Mrs. Els, some would leave their families and homes, leave behind china and favorite chairs, and follow men who seemed to fail into the endless trees and grass and mountains of the West, the mud and mice and smell of sweat. And when the men became some form of Mr. Els, comatose and starring figures of pity, then the women had to take over or become crazy. Both occurred. Mrs. Els had told me that while she waited for her husband to die, other women had come around telling her that they knew, knew what would happen and knew what she would find alone. The women patted her and murmured. Mrs. Els said at first she found no solace in this ceremony, but toward the end she came to need the feeling the women gave her, that she was just another one going either insane or into a new power.

There were more kinds of crazy too. Joshua was in good company.

I encountered Germans and Swedes and Finns who came too late or simply couldn't acquire the new language. English seemed to baffle them and leave them searching out groups who spoke their language. They clung to any shred of their old lives—flags, holidays, foods—to tolerate the West. And if they had to go abroad in the world they found themselves mystified and confused as if they had been captured and transported to an unreasonable world where all their wits counted for naught. I heard one Finn, he came to my brewery looking for work, just stand closer and closer to my foreman and yell louder and louder in Finnish as if to penetrate some magic spell that made my foreman suddenly stupid.

Compared to village life in middle Germany, every day in the West was transport to a world of the insane. So many ways—to lose wits, to have the logic of the world fail, to get your throat cut. Lovely throat.

Going after Joshua was to participate in the insane world. Staying home in Portland, taking care of businesses and appearing on the street with greetings for my fellow businessmen, banking on Thursday, eating schnitzel on Friday nights—that was the sane thing to do.

Her throat was slit like in a slaughterhouse. All her blood was soaked up by the velvet, dark, darker than a night with no stars.

Chapter Fourteen

Monsters

I was going to have to collect all the stories and rumors I could find, reliable or hysterical or apocryphal. I would be looking for a story, or rather a collection and intersection of stories that might be a man, might be a madman, might be a saint appointed by his personal god as an avenging angel to bring God's justice to earth. He might just be a mean, perverse brain injured by fever, part of a man—a monster.

I pictured him murdering Mrs. Els: as in the magazines springing up and for sale with the newspapers with drawings of lurid fiends with capes held across the face, fierce eyes, knife dripping blood. In Germany there were similar tales, usually involving partial humans that came out of the woods at night and took young people—to eat, to harm, for unclear sexual purposes. They lived in the thick darkness on the far side of the world from God's vision. I kept looking for a place in mind to store this Joshua monster, this figure in love with killing in the name of balancing out his world. All my book monsters had been a mixture of animals and people that then played out the worst of human urges unbridled by any human restraints. The animal ruled and the stories showed what could happen if our basest natures took over our lives and wrong became concentrated there.

I held theory as a way to make beer, court a wife, build a business empire, save money. I needed the compartments of theory—the best thinking on the subject—to work in my world. The West was for me a new staging ground for old theory. I tried out all things German and kept what worked: warm and cold sides in the brewery, a secret life for myself and a public life for the concocted self I used in business. I walked the streets of Portland looking for the compartments to hold Joshua, looking for a way to explain how so much blood had come out of so small a vessel as Mrs. Els. The sense was that there was no sense, and I had to enter the world without sense in order to even approach Joshua.

Now that he thought the world had been balanced out could I simply walk away, chastened, revenged upon, and live my life. In the German tradition that would have been the exact thing a reasonable German man should have done; it would be the lesson of the tale, the righteous path. I should have sighed and returned to my family, now three children, a wife, a public position, a house and servants. That was clear from the German stories.

But the West was cooking up these other stories, each with a penchant to amaze us by being out of scale and credibility for Europeans. Instead of multiple heads like classical monsters, Joshua had multiple selves in multiple places that both contradicted themselves and added together at the same time. I thought and thought about what Joshua must be, how I would confront him with actual justice, my loss of Mrs. Els, the beloved Mrs. Els.

How he would present me with his madness and fractured world, his animal that ruled him. Would I kill him or bring him to Portland justice, to public humiliation and prison and civic sponsored death by hanging? Would that make the eye for the eye? Would his death then serve the public probity?

It was a night in the eternal spring of Portland. From dead-dog streets now they were swept clean at night; slop pails dumped into the streets were forbidden. The civil contract marched onwards by small steps.

The lighted streets reminded us we were the logical extensions here of the great (and stumbling) civilizations we left behind. Each gas lamp shouted to us that we had joined Paris and London in holding back the darkness. The side streets kept secrets, kept Joshua safe while he climbed into a window…

The Portland street car lines vied with each other; on one street two different companies established in the two directions waiting for the other to fail. The evening sparked alive with the flashes of the overhead electrics. No one knew what electricity was, only that we could make and sell it, put it to work and that it would kill you if you let it. The perfect caged monster.

I walked until my feet ached. I couldn't go home until I had found the cage for my monster, the theory to contain him. It began to rain gently, with drops so small they floated up past the lights riding the heat of the city. I considered talking out this business with the doctor as I talked out my brewery plans with my eldest brewer. The doctor belonged partly to the dark world I had to enter to find Joshua. He would be a guide. He would also be a witness, and that created some problems given that I had not yet decided which solution was best for the Joshua encounter. The doctor would know more than any other person did about the whole business. I decided to take the risk since the doctor even now with his limited knowledge could do me some harm if he chose to make public my affairs.

I found him idling in his rooms after another fine meal somewhere. He was without his usual vest that strained at its buttons even before he began to eat. His cheeks were flushed with the first brandies of the evening, a cigar had gone out in the ashtray, and he wore slippers of an elaborate cloth like some wall hanging in a sultan's harem. He was glad to see me and feeling expansive and at home in the world, this evening. He offered me his best brandy, and we settled into two chairs. He knew I had something on my mind and patiently small talked until I might bring up my concern. I always believed that the doctor, as he knew more and more of my double life, became more and more circumspect and reticent about it. I also believe he knew exactly that as he knew more, he had more influence with me: that I would appreciate his confidence in useful ways for him. He was one of those men who liked the company of other men who understood an unspoken code between them, a code of protection, yes, but also of sharing the power that comes with valuable or secret information. He held his brandy up to the light to encourage me.

"I have been thinking..." I started and realized the foolishness of my own voice. I had no position, no place to be coming from, and so I stopped.

"Henry, I have seen you thinking and thinking since the death of your business partner. What are you considering?"

"I think what I would like is information about what goes on at Cumming's weekends and how Joshua fits in. I know you've said you're not sure which one he is, but maybe there is something you can tell me that might help me with...with plans to find Joshua."

"Are you sure you want that, Henry?" And then quickly, "I'm sure you have thought about this carefully. That's not what I mean. I know you are a man who thinks about things, thinks things through, I mean. But you don't know very much about Joshua or even if he was involved in her death."

"Ja, well, we..." My German accent began to grow thick as if I could cover myself in Beethoven and schnitzel until I could justify anything. "Yes of course. I don't really know, but that should never stop a man like it did in your Shakespeare's play. Not knowing. We never know, do we? And still we must do and do and do and so..." *Und zo* I heard myself saying. *Ja, und zo und zo. Na und.* "I want only to look at him, talk to him, see what I see. Can you help me find him?"

"They say he lives, when he lives with people, with Indians. That's what I know. And then there are the parts at Cummings that I only hear about, and maybe he's an important part of that."

There was a knock at the door and the doctor went to answer it, excusing himself. I couldn't see but could hear a young person's voice, boy or girl. The doctor came back and excused the interruption. I didn't ask him, and he didn't say who it was.

"I was saying," he continued, "that I only hear he has, well, some kind of peculiar tastes, ritual fancies that he likes to act out with other people. He's kind of director, as I understand it. He has people do the things he says. Personally, I'm not sure what the attraction is. I have never been invited. And I really have no interest. It sounds humiliating to me somehow."

The brandy was bringing back my confidence, the deal-maker in me. "What, good doctor, would it take to have you experiment a little, get you into the presence of Joshua and his fantasies? You could call it research? You might like it?"

"I have a better idea." He laughed. "Why don't you join me at a Cummings' event and find out for yourself? You could ask the right questions and meet Joshua I think." He was finding this immensely funny now. Brandy funny. "Now that you and Cummings are reconciled, *you* might find the whole experiment instructive, Henry. A man of your curiosities and intellect could learn something of a foreign world, a kind of thinking not part of your everyday." He was very pleased with himself. He re-lit his cigar with flourishes, a luxurious cloud of smoke like a paddlewheel steamer coming into dock. "The more I think about it, you have to admit, Henry, it's a good idea. You and Joshua meeting in the presence of other people. And other people who are participating in some ritual or ceremony lead by Joshua. Joshua the guide. Joshua the teacher.

"The monster..."

"But Henry, there are many people who qualify as monsters. Do you and I have our monster parts just under the surface of all this citizen business?"

I didn't answer for a long time. I thought there was no answer that could gather up all that blood on all that velvet, gather it up for her.

She used to hum sometimes to herself, just barely audible as if the sound were in the room and just hanging around her head. She didn't smile and didn't even seem to delight in the tune; she just hummed like a telegraph wire hummed in the wind, like a windmill pump translating the air into melody. The absence of Mrs. Els in my life was the absence of song. None of it was necessary to live, but my days were all drear without her.

The doctor and I sat for a while pondering the idea of monster. Finally I said, "I think the monster in us all is very different from Joshua because our monstrosity—mine, anyway—is so diluted with other parts: German, citizen, brewer, American, businessman, father. That's a lot of dilution, so the monster never really gets to be abroad in the world. With Joshua, he seems to have found a purer form of monstrosity unmixed with all the business I have.

Or you have. His animal nature is not watered down. Can you imagine what my beer would taste like if I sold it in concentrated form? Hops are very bitter. And the malts and sugars are not good alone. It's the watering down. I think Joshua has no good water left in him."

The doctor laughed, the brandy laughing. "God help us all if we all weren't watered down. I still think you are the one who should come to Cummings' events and find Joshua in a sort of public setting. There must be fifty people there. More sometimes."

I arrived at my house late and quietly sought out my matrimonial bed. Talk about watered down, I thought. And fell asleep.

The next week I began to lay plans to visit Cummings during one of his events. I wanted to prepare myself but I could get no specifics out of the doctor as to what I could expect, how I might prepare myself. He kept insisting that all would become clear to me once I saw what was happening. There was no way to prepare. I only needed to be alert to possibilities. I questioned him closer. He waved his hand in dismissal. He said that anything he could tell me would probably prove false to my experience once I arrived.

I decided to take along Thomas, who had been with me for many years, who had beaten Cummings, who worked his work in noiseless peace.

He was a silent young man who worked in the cooperage with shoulder muscles so developed from his

shaving of wood and banging of iron hoops, that it seemed
his head floated on the shoulders without benefit of a neck.
When he turned his head to look to the side, he created the
peculiar sensation of a head that might become separated
from his body and roll off down the sidewalk. His silence
had become legendary in the brewery. It seemed he plotted
ways each day to use as few words as possible as if some
life-force might be escaping from him with each utterance,
and he feared for his life. He might smile if you asked him
to do something, and then he might nod. And this
combination served him in the place of hundreds of words
in either German or English, both of which were employed
every day at the brewery.

As a traveling companion, Thomas was nearly perfect.
He lifted the baggage, cooked the food, cared for the
horses, spoke not a word. On the other hand, he listened if
I felt I needed to comment on the landscape or the
weather. We toiled the gentle way to Yakima on roads
more dust than mud now. Fellow travelers included local
farmers taking produce to market towns, some families
moving slowly and overburdened toward someone's dream
of land. The West had lacked the significant salt licks of
the east and central parts of the country. Once past the
mountains, settlers found alkaline ponds instead of salt
licks, fast and dangerous rivers instead of the slothful rivers
of the center and central plains. What saved the
settlements was importing salt from the ocean, something
the Indians had accomplished too. You could live as far
inland as you could carry salt to preserve your food. Salt it,

smoke it, pickle it. Sometimes I missed the fresh kills and the trade of educated butchers in Germany. Whoever would cut up a cow or goat in the West was the designated butcher, and the result was meat that spoiled and became contaminated through improper handling and storage. The German butcher was a guild member who served a long apprenticeship and learned the correct handling and storage of meats. They came to Portland but found out soon that since everyone else thought they could cut meat themselves, the profession didn't really exist. I had several German butchers working for my brewery. And since they knew the guild system, they retrained beautifully.

Thomas was not typical of the young men who came to me seeking work. He had lived in the East after a German childhood, but his father beat him, and he left home at fourteen and never looked back—not to the East, his family or Germany. When he came to me he was seeking a home for all those loyalties: to family, country, education. He began to work and found that work itself was a good home for the detached self. He was no wanderer by inclination like so many young men. He wanted to belong and belonged by loyalty and fierce work. I told him he was necessary for my journey, that he would learn important things. He nodded and prepared the wagon.

We carried two kegs of beer, provisions for several weeks and the hope that we could encounter fresh meat and vegetables on the way. Our horses were fat and smooth. We were, I was anyway, ready to slay dragons, to see the world cracked open and see what spilled out.

Cummings' weekend event, the doctor informed me, was scheduled for the next weekend, though the doctor himself said he could not attend this time.

Thomas cast his bright blue eyes about the hills up past Fort Simcoe and the first orchards where there was water. The long Yakima valley pulled water from the hills and then stood it upright in apple, peach and plum trees. We climbed the road to the sound of the harness, the thump of horses reaching into leather.

I tried to think past the slaughter of Mrs. Els, the slaughter of all innocents everywhere. The biblical man, woman and child put to the sword for nothing more than the biblical Joshua's ravings about balance in the world, equaling out the injustice and evil. Whatever concoction he believed, he believed it as fervently as a promise from God, and with religious fervor must have slit her throat and raised the steaming knife to the heavens and felt the God-given balance restored all across the waters and firmament of the earth. God's own priest, avenging angel, bringer of harmony. Did he draw the knife fast in a kind of ecstasy or slow in a lust for her life. Did he...?

I shuddered on the wagon seat and Thomas, if he felt it, said nothing but a cluck to the horses. I guessed at the fruit trees, remarked at the cloud formation, tugged my hat on tight for the wind. Mrs. Els and Joshua drawn together under western skies like elemental forces of air, water, fire...and the steel of the knife, so impartial to it all, to her lovely sadness and her laugh at sadness. What fortresses we live in to get on to the next day! Life is hard. Life is hard, chittered a grey bird in the wild rose at the side of the road.

Otto. And Mrs. Els. Why would it have been difficult to kill me and bring a smile to Joshua's God's face at how the world was rounded again and at peace? I lead an unguarded life of calculated habit. I walked the streets alone, inspected the brewing kettles, moved the scrap wood away from the wall at the back of the brewery as an example to my workers. I loved the story of Benjamin Franklin loading a wheelbarrow with papers and wheeling it down the street past his neighbors even after he had become a wealthy man. He knew the neighbors would nod their approval at his diligence, his humility, even if it was feigned. I understood Ben Franklin. It was his example that led me to the line at the Corbett bank with my bags of deposits.

I could only ferret out the order in this chaos of the West, my order, and then continue as if the world were going to stay that way, though I knew better. And so I found myself with each revolution of the wagon wheel drawn closer to the mechanism of chaos that was Joshua. He didn't kill me because there was no balance there, no eye dangling from a socket, no scar tissue to announce my turmoil to the world. He needed me to ache at the heart's core for the rest of my days. I kept thinking if I could look at him and see the deranged eyes searing off in two directions, a wild man's hair, fingers askew and arms waving at chimera and demon, then I could send that picture to hell and live out my days. I wanted him to be a flicker from the flame of hell. Then I would know. Then I could gather up my orderly life and repair to the sensible. Thomas and I would enter Cummings' debauch together. I told Thomas he must stay close when we went, he must look and remain close. That I had to confront a man about some bad business between us, and then we would leave as quickly as possible and retreat out of town. We would be unarmed. According to the good doctor, Cummings asked his guests to leave arms and knives and cudgels outside the party. If there was to be fighting it would be flesh on flesh. But the doctor also said that knives were very hard to eliminate altogether among the particular persons that gathered at Cummings.

On the road we encountered several men slouched into bone-sore riding, men who seemed to be made of the same leather as their saddles. Men headed into Yakima and apparently not related to the orchard business. Thomas watched them pass us, and I commented that these men were everywhere in the West, everywhere alone and everywhere in motion.

We camped outside of town in sight of the road to watch the parade toward Cummings' enclave. The turrets made of pointed logs, the elaborate gate decorated with fruit and corn so that each entrance sent up a celebratory flock of birds, the rooms to accommodate his guests with showers and soaking tubs, the high window above everything where he appeared regularly to check on his party guests—all some pasha's ego filling itself at the trough of the world. Cummings' parties, we learned, accounted for most of the spare cash in town that wasn't from the orchards. He must have found, besides selling my beer, some form of income to splash across the valley this way, some vein of gold somewhere. Like the famous trapper rendezvous, Cummings attracted high and low. Some camped outside his walls, especially Indians who seemed reluctant to enter until they were sure of the proceedings. And so like a circus setting up, tents and teepees rose, horses and wagons, all the while suspect men and suspect women arriving and milling and entering. From our distance we could just hear shouts and occasionally jubilant gunshots.

I had very little good information about this whole business from the doctor. Besides his reluctance to impart details about what he found attractive in the festivities, he had no other particulars either. He just said, "Oh this and that, you know. The usual and the unusual thing, of course. Just sensuality." And I assumed drunkenness to facilitate.

But when Thomas and I approached the Cummings fortress, I realized there was another thing I might have guessed—ceremony. Everywhere there were preparations and more preparations, gathering things together and separating them into piles or order. Something in the way of beginnings, and I didn't know where any of it was leading. Thomas was silent and intensely interested in the proceedings but without any notion to be fulfilled or disappointed.

An old man ground some plants against a flat rock, carefully scraping the result into a leather pouch. A dark man dressed in greasy leather was binding together reeds and cattails and coating them with what looked like tar. Several Indians sat silently against the opening of a teepee and gambled tossing small bones. Or maybe they were divining. I wasn't sure of anything but the seriousness of the action. A thoroughly wet man emerged from a doorway, clothes and hair dripping. Maybe he had bathed with his clothes on. A boy led a pair of horses past us. Three women talked and laughed sitting on logs around the remains of a fire.

Something of a fair, of a circus, of a religious holiday— the odd gathering together and the doctor's words came back to me: "Oh this and that you know. The usual and the unusual thing." I think I expected someone to be juggling recently lopped off heads and another dressed in motley catching them on spikes. I think I wanted the home-made cheeses and sausages of Lindenbronn, Wurttemberg and quilts and puppies for sale; there were none of these. And yet I got the feeling that everything I saw was for sale.

Cummings had water running into troughs for horses, even a shallow pool and several people had boots off and were cooling and biblically washing feet there. Thomas pointed out a woman who had plunked down in the center of the pool and was washing herself with great vigor, taking out each breast and cleaning it thoroughly before returning it to her wet blouse.

And everywhere was eating, some as simple as gnawing dried meat off the end of a knife. Some fires had whole carcasses roasting in coals surrounded by heaped up rocks. Thomas and I sat in the wagon just out of the action, eating cheese and bread, watching the assembly.

By evening most of Cumming's guests had moved inside the compound with stragglers still arriving. We waited until fires were lit inside and then made our way through the stockade doors. Maybe a hundred people were milling and in one corner fighting. Women seemed to be the scarce resource and these women knew the power of scarcity. A fiddler and his drumming partner kept dancers moving; some men like bears on their hind legs moved outside the paired up dancers as if waiting their turn to become human and dance with the women. My beer was everywhere—the fuel and the lubricant. Three small whiskey kegs were tapped and flowing.

The light from the fires cast shadows up the compound walls. What did Cummings get from this investment? Was this all a reward for his beer customers? Among other things that I couldn't pump out of Dr. Cruickshank was whether Cummings would ask for money sometime during the weekends, money to defray costs, for special privileges, an entrance fee. Thomas and I entered without fee. I looked to see if Cummings would make an appearance, welcome his guests. He would be unmistakable, of course, unless, like some of his guests he was affecting a disguise or a mask. There were a number of elaborate masks around, and Thomas seemed to be unable to look away from them.

High feathers swooping up from the eye holes, brightly painted sticks with skin masks on stalks, wooden pop-eyed masks like nightmares—Thomas was transfixed. Men were dressed as women. Women as men.

Not everyone was decorated or disguised, though. Most of the men and women around the whiskey barrels seemed intent on managing to get as much drink into themselves as possible. Around the beer there was a livelier crowd, so that's where we headed. I asked a woman who was laughing if she had seen our host, that I wanted to pay my respects.

"Oh you won't see him, at least for a while. He comes out like the moon. That's what he usually does, and then he disappears again. Sometimes he doesn't show his-self again at all. I think I saw him once." And she was gone, waving to someone across the crowd. I asked Thomas to wander around and see what he could see. I returned to the whiskey drinkers, thinking they were more dedicated somehow to the proceedings. I asked again after Cummings. No one knew where he was or how to find him, or said they didn't. I had the feeling I was outside looking in and couldn't quite see what was going on. Then an old trapper or mountain man or guide of some kind, sitting in the dirt motioned for me to come closer.

"You can find him yourself if you wander around upstairs. You might not like what you find. You might not find anything. That could be the best thing, too. Sit and have some of his whiskey. That's the best thing to do.

217

Take my word on that. You don't want anything to do with the black arts."

What I wanted to do was find Cummings in a room alone and have him summon Joshua and the three of us have a pow-wow on the subject of Mrs. Els and the ways of death. I don't know what I wanted. I wanted them all drawn, quartered but their skin peeled off first. I felt the seething of outrage but hadn't seen anything to be outraged about, nothing the streets of Portland hadn't already shown me. I tried the whiskey looking in its bite for some calmer thing.

After the whiskey took hold I thought I'd try the old man's advice and wander up the stairs to see what I could see. I was reminded of the biblical mansions—many rooms. Each door the same, some with soft murmurings, goings on, private acts, experiments in being human. There was light coming into the hallway from some source I couldn't directly see as if the walls were somehow lit. The urge to pop open a door and see what was happening came and then passed. I needed to listen, stop, feel into the half-light for Joshua. Or encounter Cummings making his rounds. Poor Thomas must be feeling abandoned to the revelry below.

I decided that knocking on doors, softly, judiciously, might prove useful. When I was a child we had a man in the village designated to check on doors and lock them if the property owner was negligent. The idea was that temptation was a significant part of petty crime. If someone left out a wheelbarrow, the man would tuck it inside the gate. A tool left out might be confiscated and returned at daybreak. The man was the slow son of a prominent family who had been trained to serve his people. He was re-elected every three years to fill the post again—a layer of civility and usefulness. I felt the doorknob to see if it was open. It was and I peered into the dim light.

There were three people on a pallet, three that I could see. Maybe more. All were naked. I closed the door.

After being reminded of the door man of my village, after closing the door on the tangle of sweating people of various genders, I waited in the hall for sounds to guide me, and my mind wandered again to Lindenbronn. The road came in from the east through the woods and left to the west through the fields. In the village were about ten families. There were fewer people in Lindenbronn than in Cumming's compound.

The sexual union of humans and animals was not unknown to me. I had read in German of such things; I had the stories of Hoffmann, of course, the magical transformations that took place between humans and animals. And once they could become one another, sexual congress was the next step, then the offspring and mixing of the elemental with the complexity of humans.

Toward the end of the hallway I passed a man leading a goat and a sheep. Did the union of man and beast have a soul? A mind? Was Joshua a beast? What was the offspring of a woman and a demon? St. Augustine wrote that God creates souls and then infuses them into a child about 45 days after conception. Proprietary information, it always seemed to me. Hebrew scholars believed God made the great flood to sweep away the monsters, giants and fallen angels that resulted from iniquitous sex between women and all manner of polluted being. Myself, I took the brewer's view of this world. There was a logic to anything if closely examined, the same logic that gave us beer—this goes with that: warm mash, cool storage, sugar to hops. All things could be discovered and controlled if you were patient and diligent. The West of America held many surprises for a young German man, but this young German man brought some things to the West too. He brought the reason of a small town and the belief of his religious people.

So then I found myself walking a dim hallway with livestock that was being lead to sexual misadventure. The sheep bleated and balked. The goat looked on amused. The floor of the hallway was suddenly thick with the fragrant mess of both their bowels as if they anticipated some need to empty them on the floor before the festivities.

I thought of my grandfather's tales of what he called "the days when there were witches everywhere in Germany." He would slowly tell the tales, reluctantly as if it might not be a good idea; he would make us begin to whine a little for the scary lore, and then he began.

"They were not all women, you know." And he'd stop to light his pipe. Tobacco clouds were part of witchcraft in my memory, and then the fire of the match, the throat clearing. He had no tales of sexual congress with animals, no version of Cummings's hallway. "But most of them were, you see. And the women were the most powerful kind. The bible tells us that. The bible witches were mostly women too. And when I was a young boy in this country, there were everywhere people to be very careful about. Most would not look to interfere with a young person who behaved himself, but if there was a rascal or a scoundrel, *ein Lausbub*, then it always seemed that a witch became enraged and harmed them. My grandfather believed that a good supply of witches in a town was the best sort of civil protection—against meddlers and scoundrels, against gossips and malicious people without enough to do with their hours. Against children behaving badly." Here he would rekindle the pipe to let the message sink in. Here he invoked five generations of family as witness to the wisdom of his story. And then he was off on transformation, flying, possession, mushroom mischief, transposed souls of humans and animals. In short, my grandfather has his own version of E.T.A. Hoffman stories, reminding me that Hoffman, like the brothers Grimm, really only harnessed some versions of the folk tales found everywhere in the German people. And in the case of the brothers, they went to no greater inconvenience than to poll their middle class neighbors for versions to use. But my grandfather thought the genius, the truths, the historical verities always came from the folk: with their quilt patterns, their local speech peculiarities, their respect or contempt for political and economic boundaries.

The hallway at Cummings's emptied, and susurrations from behind the doors were almost inaudible. I walked on expecting maybe my grandfather, his grandfather, around the corner.

I prowled the hallways that first night listening for I-don't-know-what. Some kind of action that might involve Joshua and Cummings, something worse than I was able to imagine maybe. What I saw would have been predictable had I taken the time to think it through—orgies and animals and sweat and liquor, moaning and shouting and laughing. How unimaginative, unattractive is the human sexual congress. Without providing a great deal of extra equipment—and I suppose animals qualify here—there seem to be only a limited range of what who can do to whom, and it doesn't seem to really matter what genders are in combination: the human equipment seems to limit what can be done, and then done again. That's the physical side. On the emotional side, of course, the variety is endless, and this is where people get hurt.

At my houses, working with Mrs. Els, we considered what was allowable and what might be allowable if the women consented and got paid extra. It was all a logical business transaction, after all. And for the most part, the clients wanted predictability the same things in the same way—the basics. Certain more demanding men Mrs. Els caught early on in the dealings and arranged events to their peculiarities with the understanding that there were limits and implied promises and stipulations. Again I think of making beer as the best metaphor—the reasonableness of it all.

Late that first night, finding only more and more of the same, I yawned and went to find Thomas who had fallen asleep against a pillar in the courtyard. I would like to say the wilderness howled around us, but it didn't. The festivities wound down like the dying campfires, warm ashes, some orange glows deep down.

The next day we took the horses out to a pasture and rented them a few hours grazing while I pondered some strategy to reveal Joshua without being a bad guest or getting us in trouble with the participants. I arrived at a plan in which I engaged our host in an inquiry that...

Thomas raised both eyebrows at once as if I had proposed an immensely stupid thing—watering the beer, using rotten hops—some roundly thick thing that was so clearly wrong that nature itself complained. At least in Thomas-the-silent that's what I sensed. I stopped articulating my plan and waited for him to supply some corrective. Thomas whittled himself a toothpick, knowing he would have to speak. He began by telling what he had overheard. He spoke slowly in German. He said he had heard some at this fire, some at that during the evening. Then he had moved from drinking group to drinking group and even had been invited into what he called "the rooms of iniquity." That sounded biblical to me, and I waited. I waited for him to tell me if he went, of course, but it seemed that he didn't even consider it a possibility and found no reason to include a denial in his story. He said that he had heard that Cummings and Joshua, that Joshua principally and then Cummings as a point of contact between Joshua's wilderness and the Yakima Valley, that Joshua had brought to the parties an endless supply of wealth—gold—that he somehow got with the aid of the Indian tribes. He even heard that Cummings's beer buying and selling was a fraudulent front that made Joshua's wealth seem to be only a story, a story that had no roots in reality and so no pursuers trying to find the source of the gold. Joshua came and went secretly. I suggested that all this might have been just talk, some of the regulars trying to account for the lavish and free spectacle. But Thomas said again that he heard nearly the same thing from the oldest regulars—that the gold was endless, that Joshua was considered a magician or holy man by the Indians, that Cummings was just a useful pipe through which Joshua could conduct his wealth, could turn his wealth to his own ends. As with the Indians, Joshua couldn't eat gold.

I liked the idea of Joshua dependent on civilization for his perversions to fructify. I even pictured his contempt for what Cummings had reported as the imbalance of the world that needed to be set aright. I pictured a madman raving in the wind, in the filth of his golden wealth, in the face of God's contempt for an empty and vicious life. I recalled the Hammurabi code and its insistence that there indeed was an equal and available eye for every eye, tooth for every tooth. And there was Joshua the self-appointed administrator, judge, of eternal justice. I needed to hate him like a man hates a man, but I kept encountering some

historical abstraction, some figure that always was in the
landscape of time. And that figure didn't have blood and
bones, just meaning, some construed and social sense of
how the human worked. Joshua was like a cave painting in
the wildness of the West.

Cummings's fair continued the next day without
stopping—only the embers dying down. But soon the fires
were back up and roasting things in endless supply. People
had to eat. Thomas had discovered a pen of chickens that
was one of the public food supplies, apparently endlessly
refurbished. The guests only had to come to the gate to be
given one for each hand. Deer hung in a row from an X-
brace and these too could be carried off whole or in pieces,
and again there seemed no end to the resupply. I admired
the organization of the provisions, the chain of command
like a military fort with re-supply sergeants.

Hunters arrived with more deer. A farmer unloaded
crates of chickens. Beer by midday was re-lubricating the
social contract. Where were the principles, the host? We
asked around again and found a number of guests who
didn't really recognize Cummings's name and had no idea
of Joshua. But there were some who only had praise for
Cummings and hushed silence for the specter of Joshua.

I was intrigued by the hushed silence. It was
somewhere in that silence that the fear was. I had the
feeling I was opening a door, passing over to the other side.
The other, just over there through that veil and you'll find
the signs and symbols are different, the signifying flayed
open and the blood-wet interior exposed. I had come to

the West seeking an idea, a German ideal of traveling back
in time to when land was plentiful and people few—the
opposite of my childhood's Germany. That ideal included
only a few of the many consequences of the wild, the pre-
reasonable, the blank slate that could be written on any way
the writer could, like writing on water.

I stood and watched one day, when I was new to
Oregon, a young man snagging salmon with a large treble
hook. He'd gaff them out of the plentitude of the
Willamette River and toss them onto the bank into a heap
of flopping. He had maybe twenty fish, more than he
could carry on horseback; he'd need a wagon. But an old
sorrel stood by, its reins tossed into a bush, a ragged cloth
saddle bag drooping from one side. And still he heaped up
the fish, probably because he could. I was reminded of the
gulls that fed on the salmon flies during a hatch. They had
filled their stomachs but something in the feeding reflex
made them stay in the sky striking and striking but not
swallowing fly after fly so that the air rained salmon fly eggs
and wings and thoraxes and legs.

And the boy couldn't stop either. He was snagging a
fish on every throw of his hook, wrenching the fish
sometimes tail first onto the sand. Because he could.
Because the fish offered themselves in such obscene
excess, and like a king's overflowing counting house, the
river yielded treasure after treasure.

I asked him what he was going to do with all those fish.
His eyes were glazed over, and he tossed the hook again. I
repeated the question; he was in a feeding frenzy where

only lust for more seemed to be operating. Maybe he had tapped that urgent longing that we are at base, that thing that wants to eat and live and nothing more complicated. Finally he slowed, tossed again after unhooking another fish, looked at me as if I had just arrived in his vision. What? He seemed to say. Throw, hook, heave onto the pile. Two fish were flopping toward the river, making a break for it. He ignored them. It was the catching that lifted him, not the having. Then he stopped, peeved at my interruption. He looked at me. "What am I going to do with them?" His voice was husky with treasure. "I'm...I'm going to take them...home. Then, I don't know. I'm going to take them home."

My first Germans I met in America said essentially the same thing about the largess: of land, of possibility, of wealth. They talked of taking all this home, to Germany. Take home wealth, position, excess and loudness and gesture and chaos. And, of course, home would have none of it. Though some tried and paraded themselves through the streets of their villages with some valuable bauble, some New World excess like a horse saddle or a gold chain of office (without the office). And here at Cummings's there was with the meat and liquor the same sense of piled excess and no particular thing to do with it but slurp and gnaw and ask for salt.

The bones collected around one of the largest fires, the bone fire, and crackled under foot. Lean dogs that had been darting in the first day—snouted divers from the edges—the second day trotted from one fire to the next picked up a bone, discarded it for another, slouched off to digest in the shade. Thomas told me he had seen coyotes mixing with the dogs in the evening as the light faded, cashing in on shared ancestry. Crows and black birds sat prominent, bounced away from the scuffling feet and returned. The second day the feasting had lost its frenzy and now the feasters consummated meat, celebrated my beer, blessed the bounty and the benefactors in slowed down ritual feeding and sleeping. They started again, so that by noon we were witnessing another round of indulgence and sloth and gluttony and... Biblical sins. The sins of monstrous human longing.

The sins of Joshua. I had told Thomas the tales of the various Joshuas I'd heard, the saintly, the satanic: avenging angel, St. Francis called away from his garden glade. Thomas asked me which side I thought was the true Joshua. I told him that both of them were the concentrated biblical versions of humans that were Joshua. All monstrosity is about excess and bad proportion, and the scale of measurement is human comfort. These people had come to Cummings's fortress for the monstrous, the antidote to the scratch and scrabble of the rest of their lives in the West among giant, wet trees and dry rocks, deep and thrumming rivers, bears and cougars that would eat their children. The West was a fairy tale come slouching off the page dragging behind it all the horrors of fairy tales, all the unlikely compression that the brothers Grimm found so German, so telling about the people who lavished these stories on their children. But the real version of bears and dark objects cursing the wind, slithering into beds at night, luck gone sour, beauty gone inhospitable, the real version was this sweating coupling of men and women in fear and ecstasy at the same time, the smell of orifices and semen. The stuff of the beginning of the world. And the end. All acted out with some kind of theatrical regularity at Cummings's.

I couldn't help thinking how in Germany Fasching contained all this business, this license and foolishness and danger, kept it between two dates and allowed the people to court excess and their hidden sentiments and curiosities—kissing and fornicating and...

But Cummings, this second day, suddenly made an appearance on a balcony and waved his hand in a benediction. What was this blessing worth? This unholy Pope of an Irishman disfigured. Bad businessman (until lately, it seems) and generous host—what were his lips forming there on the balcony?

Cummings—I don't know if anyone in the compound could hear him from that height, and he didn't shout—was joined by a young woman in a long, red shawl. She stood up straight, the top of her head reaching to his shoulder. His arm went around her shoulder and pulled her close. Still he spoke and gestured as if from some mountain top, and I think that no one heard. He seemed to pantomime for about twenty minutes sawing the air with his free arm, circling it over his head as if to suggest a halo, acting out some iconography of one-eyed power, calling on gods, invoking spirits, quoting scripture, calling up the devil—

who knows? I don't know. Maybe all of those. How odd of him to play on the silent charade.

I sent Thomas closer near the beginning of the speech to see if he could hear from directly below. Thomas came back to me shaking his head. He couldn't hear Cummings's voice. He must be speaking in a hushed whisper so only his companion could hear. Maybe he was claiming all this—celebrants, feasting, drinking, sleeping—as his own. Suzerain and master, supplier of chickens and fire, god of plenty and surfeit—Cummings could have been blessing us all.

Then the woman left his side and disappeared into the dark behind him. But Cummings remained motionless, his hands on the railing, as if breathing in the nectar of his creation.

Somewhere back inside there and down those corridors and in those rooms and under some bed and maybe in a hole in the wall, somewhere was Joshua gestating for the evening's activities.

Mrs. Els used to tell me how painfully thin she was as a child. Her mother and aunts forced food on her constantly, and she ate constantly but grew no fatter. Finally they gave up since she was never sick and at play was the leader of the gang of children in the neighborhood. She thought her mother must have believed she would live forever, she laughed. Then her husband, when he grew ill, told her how much he depended on her. And then he took to staring out the window at the woods, waiting for something to come and mercifully take him away. I pictured her slaughter again, the ritual bloodletting to balance the world and eat out the core of my heart.

Why am I here watching Cummings like some carved cuckoo come out of the clock and then, confused, planting himself on the railing and refusing to go back in as if he could stop the time, the ticking? Why am I not walking the hallways with a very large knife in my belt looking for revenge, simple tooth-for-a-tooth revenge? Why am I not scouring out the holes in the walls that hide Joshua, the Joshuas, and cutting their throats again and again?

Beer always saves me: the logic of beer and beer making.

Thomas and I retire from the courtyard to outside the walls. The horses ask to be seen to. The cheese we brought is excellent. The evening requires a plan. And we'll need fresh, well fed horses for the trip home.

The weather change is a surprise and comes over the hills quickly into the valley. There is threat in the clouds and the sudden silence of the birds. A flock of quick, small birds flies off almost as one and disappears into a thicket of oaks. I am pleased by the portentous nature of the weather, but Thomas is more interested in protecting our food and transportation from the possible storm. Practical Tom. A horse in a thunder storm is always a test of horse mettle, a kind of challenge to the character of beast, asking it to separate the duty of serving the wagon and the masters from its nature to seek shelter out of the storm. A dark cloud brews itself slowly, I imagine mostly hidden by the high hills, its bulk ascending the back side for an assault on the Yakima Valley. I find metaphor everywhere. I hear Beethoven in my head but don't discuss the music with Thomas.

After a while it begins. Both the storm and the festivities of the second evening have commenced theatrically. The light is changed since the storm took the afternoon sun and caged it in black producing the yellow-gray disc paused, hanging above the hills. I think I will not leave this valley the same man I came in. I think I might be a fugitive from the law and have to steal back to Germany empty handed. I know I will be emptied out of this worm that turns in my heart.

I also know that reality comes in layers and the layers we see easily are the most false. That the layers we have to wait to see, that reveal themselves to us when we are ready to see, those layers are more fiercely real and change us utterly. It's not just that I am German and inclined to the fraudulent order of life and then surprised by the power of the other worlds. It's that I have become a western American and live with the battle of realities every day: the banks and steamships and railroads, the Mr. Els kind who seem to empty out into the unforgiving wildness, the bears who wander into town and stand on their hind legs for a while and then go back into the woods.

The rain began thoroughly wetting the valley without much wind. Thomas and I remained sheltered against it until the festivities seemed to have begun in earnest. Cummings was nowhere to be seen when we entered the compound, and the fires tended by celebrants had been moved out of the rain but dangerously close to the wood under the balconies. Thomas pointed out again that several coyotes had come into the compound with the resident dogs following the trail of cooking meat and the smell of grease. Smaller animals scampered out of the shadows momentarily, snatched at crumbs and disappeared again. The dust of the compound began to turn to mud and stick to our boots like pasty brewery waste. I expected the god Pan to appear from behind a log pillar, smile at the proceedings, give his blessing and slink into the darkness to join in.

I stood with Thomas for a while watching the firelight take over from the storm light, the shift through the last fizzled sun to the fires of night. A pillar caught on fire and was quickly doused by two men who then scraped the fire away from the building where it hissed in the rain. I kept shaking my head at the signs and chuckling until Thomas asked me what I thought was funny there.

"Oh Thomas, I think I have come so far in this short life that I am being captured by my own story. I see everywhere the fire and the rain. I didn't used to."

Thomas said he saw fire and rain too, but we meant different things.

I told him I'd look for him later, that he was to stay alert for signs of Joshua activity and then do nothing but come for me.

I tried the same hallways as the night before, just to make sure I had not missed something. It was early in the evening and if the pattern held up, the activity would build as the light left the sky. I wondered again what the nature of this business would be. An old bowed man with a long fire wand came along the corridor silently lighting lanterns and hanging them on the walls. So tonight was to be the illuminated version of last night. I hoped for illumination myself.

I got my first ritual vision of Joshua across an immense room, a room that seemed too large to fit into the building. The light coming from one side cast long shadows that danced like dark fire with every movement. What are they doing? What I could see did not help me.

Cummings was the ringmaster, I think. I think there was a small commotion on the right side and then stillness there. I think the light came and went in brightness, and that was a problem with my seeing. A figure in the back like a priest but dressed in greasy buckskin, a bearded and fierce-haired atavistic brute-man—that's what I thought later. I rounded out the image I couldn't see. I was sure it Joshua or the Joshuas of my westering. It was not the Joshua of the high fever and sunken cheeks. But it might have been the silent Joshua who then walked off into the woods to heal.

Cummings was talking in a low voice and I realized the low light made him even harder to hear. He gestured to the shadow that had produced Joshua.

"...a full loaf, a voice from the wild..."

Cummings seemed to be introducing Joshua, but the buckskin bear with wild hair and beard seeking out the biblical seemed to take no notice. The light played lower still. I thought I might make my way through the adherents, the acolytes, the audience—I didn't know what I was seeing. And it occurred to me how much of the time in my life I didn't know what I was seeing.

I thought I should not let my mind wander away from exactly what was happening in front of me. I needed to belong to the moment. Where was Thomas?

Joshua (I was still assuming I was seeing Joshua) began to bellow: low and like a bull across a field, then higher but with the low sound still intact and suddenly symphonic. He began to wave his hands in the air as if to get rid of something hot stuck to his fingers. Cummings backed to the wall and Joshua assumed the center.

I was thinking they had worked out the theater there and were after some effect that was largely lost on my German skepticism. This business was not meant for me to witness. I was the audience to a play I didn't understand, so I looked to the others to guess what they were understanding. I remember being very clear that I was not afraid of anything happening, as if I'd made up my mind to end existence here and simply watch it happen. I would let the thing eat me up.

I couldn't tell, I couldn't see, I was not part, I didn't understand or, I realized, I didn't want to. Some dead thing was being dragged into the light. I was sure it was dead by its mass and inertia. How scientific! Maybe it was a cow or a deer. I couldn't see the head part. The woman next to me was sweating so fiercely that it dripped off the end of her nose onto her breasts. Someone behind me bumped me and his heavy breathing took over the air around me. Two naked people came out of the crowd toward the dead thing. Joshua flicked and raged. Cummings crossed his arms on his chest and seemed content with whatever was happening.

As the two people tangled together across the beast, the Joshua chanted, the light flickered, the room became oppressively hot and moist. I, who had been the strangest of strangers, began to feel oddly bored with whatever sexual ritual I was seeing. I wanted to point out the obvious—there was a dead thing and on top of it were two live things. Now three. Maybe four. I wanted Joshua in a room in my brewery, a meeting, a hanging, a reckoning. I didn't want this room, this sweat, this breathing. I am a reasonable man and wanted reasonable, Old Testament revenge. This naked body, that brown slaughtered thing, the priest's incantation, the person behind me rubbing now on my backside, the light, the dark.

I spun around then found myself walking slowly back down the corridor putting out the lanterns. I was shaking my head. I had stayed, apparently, for only part of something: the dead part, the sex part. Not only did I not understand, I was no longer curious what kind of circus Cummings had invented in these woods, these orchards. I wanted to sit on the bed with Mrs. Els and talk and talk and talk. About nothing. And more nothing, the ephemera of the day and night, and so last until the end of my life with no more meaning than good beer.

I looked for Thomas in the compound. I listened to hear Joshua's bellowing but couldn't hear from down here. I sought the whiskey barrel; the arthritic man who couldn't get up who sat nearby and medicated his joints. When I went out into what was left of the rain, there was still no Thomas at the wagon. What had I asked him to do except to be around? Was I going to suddenly avenge myself on the hairy woods dweller I was still calling Joshua? Shoot him?

I felt like an old man searching in a dim room for somewhere to sit down. I was looking for signs. What to do? The rain withheld any comment whatsoever. The compound floor had become slick mud to match the sweat and the greasy buckskin Joshua had posed in.

A truth came to me slowly that I should simply go back to Portland, find some strong men and true who would do an ugly job for a lot of money and have them simply remove Joshua from the earth and sky and the woods as Mrs. Els had suggested. The minute I paid them I could slap my hands together and be rid of this thing. I wouldn't even care if they killed him or crippled him or what. If they fed him to wolves and bears. If they sold his scalp to some superstitious bumpkin who used it as a sexual talisman. Where is Thomas? I want to talk to him about this. I want him to listen to me talk about this, and then we'll go home following the rumps of those gracious horses. I want, I want I want.

What had I suspected I could find out at Cummings's party? What newness that I couldn't imagine did I think I'd find? Why was the sex and sweat and heat so old, not new? So boring? I should have realized the good doctor was trying to tell me I wouldn't find much of interest there. Not what he found in Cummings's back rooms and dim light. I don't think he could have been more clear, but he only said what he could and then stayed away himself. I think he knew that I didn't know what I would do if I found Joshua. My new plan to seize Joshua by the scruff of his neck, by proxy, by contract, now seemed the business-like thing to do. I had, after all, a great many duties to my community, the German Guild, my money and my family and my brewery.

Thomas came to the wagon silent and covered in blood.

Chapter Fifteen

Homeward

After a time—I let him find his explanation in his own time—he told me haltingly as if dredging some pit for the information, that he had too much to drink and was asked to help with the hanging and slaughter of some deer and had opened a deer's neck to bleed it, and it got on himself when he slipped in the mud. I advised him to go back to the compound and wash in the spigot there, but he said no. We could stop by the river on the way out of the valley, and he'd wash there. There would be no sense in traveling by the night road in the wet. We could leave in the morning, first light. Thomas said he would find the river tonight since it wasn't far, and wash there and be back. I slept and didn't hear him come back but he was cleared of blood in the morning.

We left and the road was empty but for us. The orchard flowers were gone and the mud pink with fallen petals, and we left brown tracks in the pink road while the petals had drifted from the trees.

All the way home the silent Thomas fell even more silent as if he had gone deep into the cave of himself and slept there rolled into a ball like any bear. He sat the wagon seat stolidly, reins in hand with his gaze fixed over the horses' heads. Instead of his usual clucking to the beasts he twitched the reins on their backs when they slowed on a hill or in mud or fell to plodding in rhythm with each other, their familiar head wagging and nudging each other like two huffing gossips. Thomas was animated only to pull his hat on tighter when the wind came up. I could have held better conversation with a keg of beer.

We had been back a week when Thomas happened to pass me in the brewery with nothing but his customary nod. I returned to my office and reconsidered again his story about the blood bath he'd received. He had heard me talk about Joshua. Did he know what I thought Joshua had done? The doctor did. The doctor could easily have told Thomas to look out for me and what he feared I might do at Cummings's. What was the possibility that Thomas had taken his own silent revenge for me? Waited for Joshua after the mooing and sweating show, waited and cut his throat in my name? All the way back on the road I talked of nothing that happened that night. I spoke of beer. Thomas said nothing to me, only hummed to the horses when he relieved them of harness each night on the return trip. I don't know why I thought no more of his blood bath. Thomas toiled diligently for me bringing barrels and barrels of beer to my bank accounts, earning his pay. Would he have anticipated my wanting to know that Joshua was no longer walking the woods and bellowing to the satanic unwashed?

Thomas was old fashioned about the boss-worker relationship. In Germany the boss was more of the patron, the father. The worker was the protected one, the child, the plant that owed its life to the sun. In order to find out whether he had done my revenge for me in the name of this loyalty, I had asked him repeatedly where the blood came from, what he had done. And he repeatedly demurred and said he didn't know what I wanted him to say. Had he killed Joshua? He didn't know who Joshua was, what he looked like. Had he killed someone he thought might be Joshua? He hadn't killed anyone. Had he beaten, then, someone who might have been Joshua even if he didn't know what Joshua looked like?

And then he looked at me as if I had said something childish—in German much worse for a grown man to be childish than in English—and asked if he could get back to working. To working for me, to earning his daily bread and mine.

I had to wait to get word from Dr. Cruikshank the next time he traveled to Cummings's event. I had to wait after that to hear from men I sent out to talk to the Indians around Cummings's fortress. Neither had any news about Joshua. But he sometimes, the men had heard, sometimes just disappeared off into the woods for a time, and no one heard from him, not Indian or White. Thomas passed back and forth in my brewery—cold side, warm side—his gait like the draught horses steady and certain the way he placed his feet on the ground.

The good doctor, on the other hand, had nothing but speculation for me: some had said that Joshua couldn't be killed, and I shouldn't worry, a man he met had seen someone shoot at Joshua point blank with no effect, the

Indians considered him a ghost from the spirit world. In his own mind he must have seen himself as an avenging angel, a messenger from God, a righter of wrongs and a maker of the crooked to be straight. What is so fierce as self-righteousness? Mine? His?

Mrs. Els often wanted me to take her out of the city, especially to one place near the Willamette River above the falls. There was a long bend in the river that changed the flow from south to more than west. We could only see one segment of the river there, like a lake. The surface was glass and protected by trees perfectly reflected in the water. A swimming animal, maybe a beaver or otter left the bank to enter the river. She sat looking for a long time at the river as if trying to read something there, some glyph on the rock bank, something stone would reveal only to her. I watched her puzzle out the secrets with her head cocked like any river bird.

She liked to sit silently like this. Then she put her hand on my knee and said, "Henry? Do you ever want to just leave your body and mix back in with everything? Do you think that's allowed?"

She always joked about what might be allowed in the West, how maybe there were new rules that we hadn't stopped to consider when we came west. I would play with her like my mother did with my father and say I thought we were making up everything, making the world for the first time. Like Adam and Eve.

"Ah, that's what I mean," she said. "There were rules, but they didn't follow them."

I defended the first mother and father. I said that God
was not clear enough about those rules. God was being
stingy with the best parts of the garden giving them naming
rights and a couple other things, but not the really good
stuff, the stuff that would have them both know what they
were doing there. The rules were a cheat.

"So God is capable of cheating?" She folded her hands
in her lap and looked back to the river.

"I think God is capable of anything, even cheating.
He's God. That's how we made him up."

"He can sit my husband at the window and slowly
empty him out thought by thought?"

"He can. I think he can because He does."

"You are so sure, Henry? Why?"

"Because I left God in Germany in a small church in
Lindenbronn painted white and yellow. I thought it would
be a good place for God, that my father's neighbors would
take good care of him there."

"And not your father?"

"My father had left God somewhere too, a long time
ago. I don't know where, and some of the children were
too young to tell yet. I thought he might tell me, but he
never did." She watched the river; it seemed she was always
watching the river in some way. I thought she might be
thinking of her husband, how the West, not God, sucked
the juices right out of him. I could never tell what she was
thinking. Once I said something like, I know you're
thinking…, but she stopped me and slowly let me know
that I didn't, I didn't know what she was thinking. And

that was all. She just looked at me to make sure I knew that the look was enough. It was. What she was thinking was entirely proprietary, and she owned it utterly.

The Joshua silence became palpable. I began to send messages with my delivery men: messages to the north to Cummings, messages to the Indians, but that was always more difficult—they didn't owe me a cent and had no reason to send anything back but more silence. From Cummings I eventually received the same message I got elsewhere, that Joshua often disappeared for long periods of time. He came and went on some schedule all his own. I wanted to ask Cummings if anyone suspected…well, anything regarding Joshua, but just phrasing the question or myself made it sound stupid. Cummings with his one eye, the other sewn shut and monstrous anywhere else but the West where one-eyed men and one-legged and one armed men were common. The price of being here, I thought. It's what needs to be paid. The blood sacrifice.

In time I began to give up on Joshua-news and then only listen to the tales of new madmen who lived in the woods. There are always new madmen and women living in whatever woods wherever. They are the mad people who live inside us.

I had more difficulty ridding myself of Mrs. Els. My businesses, my daughters, the German Foundation, the Portland streetcar commission, the brothers Corbett, and, of course, beer, always beer—did not sufficiently distract me from the blood that flowed out of Mrs. Els.

Chapter Sixteen

The Rest

The rest of the story must come in pieces. Thomas was attacked at night by a desperate man who could not have seen clearly the size and strength of Thomas. The man jumped out of the dark and clubbed Thomas across the back of the head knocking him down. But when the man began to go through Thomas's pockets, Thomas arose like the wrath of God (I imagined) and then, Thomas said, he simply hurled the attacker into a stone wall, there was a loud snapping sound. The man was killed immediately, his back broken. Thomas carried the body for over a mile to find the police and tell his story. They kept Thomas until they could determine who he was, who the dead man was (or wasn't, it turned out. They could never find a name for him. From his hands they decided he had worked in the woods.).

This might have been the end of any trouble for Thomas since he was a citizen and worked for me, and the dead man had been an empty sack. But again, this time in a bar, a respectable bar, Thomas had stopped for a beer and someone, the reason was not clear—this time it wasn't robbery—jumped on his back as he stood at the bar. Thomas had simply flung the man from him, but again the force was so great that the man died of multiple broken bones.

Two deaths became more of a problem for the police. They declared Thomas a "dangerous person," like the petty criminals they caught in multiple crimes, like the sneak thieves and pickpockets, the con men and cheating gamblers. These dangerous persons were taken to the edge of town, released and asked not to return. The penalty for returning was jail and hard labor.

Thomas appealed to me. I went to the judge, to the police. I pleaded bad luck on the parts of the two attackers. I asked why anyone in his right mind would attack someone the size of Thomas. I brought Thomas's work record, his promotions, his daily habits of contributing to the welfare of the people of Portland. I enlisted the German Development Committee who wrote a testimonial to Thomas as a good citizen of Portland. Thomas was spared exile, but the implied promise the police extracted from him was that he would avoid fights (he claimed not to really have been in any fights—just the single gesture of throwing off an attacker). I overheard two of my employees later talking about Thomas in hushed tones and calling him "killer," only half joking.

Silent Thomas, who had friends at work because of his peaceful good nature, found himself in a kind of exile maybe worse than being taken to the edge of town by the police. I made a point of always talking to him as I passed through the brewery on my inspection tours, always making sure the rest of the men saw that Thomas was not only in my favor but a worker whose opinion I valued and sought out. Still every day brought greater distances between

Thomas and his world: work, society, friendship. The exile grew.

I began to speculate more about the gore-covered image I had of Thomas that evening in Yakima. Had something spectacularly bloody happened that night and Thomas remembered it only partially or not at all? Had there been the hanging of the deer, then some equivalence of the attacks in which Thomas's prodigious strength had ripped open the logic of the world?

I must admit that my time in the new world—a young man growing old—had prepared me in ways no Hoffmannesque stories could for great cracks in the surface of the world into which a man might slide at any moment, down, down into dark magic and opaque miracle with scattered, flimsy reason blowing away. I had become an old man who felt the surface of life was an elaborate fraud, an elaborate and fragile fraud. Mrs. Els just through the veil of daily deceit, just over there where she still laughs in the amber light of the steamboat window, still reaches over to touch my knee by the river with spring light and live water, and at the same time empties her life out onto the velvet, minute after horrible minute. They were all happening every day, all the time, over and over.

Thomas picks up some man and throws him completely to the stars.

As the story gets closer to my telling it, everything about it becomes less clear. I have tried to render the Joshua part in somewhat biblical terms, my way of

understanding it. His name could have been Robert and
the bible might never have entered into the telling. I think
now that the Joshua imperative for the name came from all
the tellings and retellings of the stories, and the tellers
settled on Joshua because…well, because of Jericho,
because of heroism and the slaughter and the finger of God
implied. I think maybe Robert might have made a cleaner
story.

Joshua was not killed by Thomas. Joshua did not kill
Mrs. Els.

How much clearer could it be? I made more and more
money selling beer and less and less on the girls as the
twentieth century began. My instincts were right: beer was
the essential truth, the long-run truth. God made water
and then humans made beer as a contribution to a
celebration of God's water. That was finally what I know
for sure.

Joshua lived by eating the earth as close to dirt as
possible they said. He ate roots unclean and small pebbles.
They saw him warm his meat on a fire and then eat it. He
ate bark and lichens and the inside of bark like a beaver.
They reported that he was always chewing on something—
when he came, when he stayed, when he left. He chewed
the uneatable until it became food for him. His hunger was
perfect. They said… They? Who were they?

The first reports of Joshua at home in his lair came
from Indians who had gone to find him and draw him out
of the forest into their camps to heal them. Small pox, the

white scab, measles, the red death for their children. Though he could do nothing for them they thought he might be able to drive off whatever evil brought these plagues down on them. They said he made them all wash their hands and faces over and over until they were raw. Then wash everything they owned until the camp was wet and scrubbed. Then he left. That was the first they.

The next they were settlers who ran cattle in the woods in the summer and encountered Joshua—the Joshua of Cumming's events, anyway—moving through the morning or evening light, usually away from them like a wary animal. When they spoke to him they saw him eating and confirmed the hunger in his story. Some offered him the warmth of their fireplaces, their cooked food and talk, but they said he was polite and refused and melted back into the woods.

I wanted to see this Joshua for myself and set out on horseback and alone this time to find him. I told my family I was looking for some land north of Portland as a railroad investment. I would be gone about two weeks. A single horse and my curiosity to unwind the braided rope that was his story, a rope, I found, that had braids inside the braids so that each unwinding revealed that strand too was made of cunning windings.

I had been traveling for ten days and wondering why I had not again engaged Thomas to travel with me: to listen to my speculations on the world, to care for the horses and cook. But after ten days the voices that made me do the right, the German *pflichte* thing, they became calm and then

silent, and I moved into the woods and worked the edges
like lace, weaving into the darkness seeking Joshua and
then out into the grasslands the Indians had burned to keep
them open for hunting. In and out, stitches. I grew dirty.
I drank water with my face plunged into the stream that
came from the wooded hillside. I lost the cup I had
brought to dip water. I lost a number of things: the small
ropes I used to keep camping equipment tied to the saddle,
the trade beads and knife blades I brought to greet all
Indians, the parchment paper I used to wrap leftover food
in the saddle bag, the wool scarf I wrapped around my neck
against both sun and cold, the heavy work gloves, the brass
compass. I seemed to grow careless, but what really
happened was that these things became unnecessary, and I
simply left them sitting where I had unpacked them for the
evening. I got up each day unburdened a little more. I
realized, saw clearly what was happening but had no will to
stop it.

The trail led north, so I went north. The trail
disappeared on rock, and I never looked for where it
continued. I took to the woods more and more because the
trees were farther apart and beneath them was a hospitable
park that at midday smelled of vanilla from the bark of the
tall pines. I became sure that I was no longer looking for
Joshua but just riding out and out. When the park-like
terrain gave way to steeper and more difficult game trails, I
veered back into the park and continued to travel wherever
the pleasant land might lead me. There seemed no sense in
going where the path was difficult simply because it was

difficult. I had to remind myself I was looking for someone. But I also thought that I would or would not find Joshua based not on where I went so much as the mere fact of going. Then it occurred to me that the less that occurred to me the more happened. I laughed.

The summer sun cooked the trees and the vanilla smell was powerful. My horse seemed drunk on it. We stopped for water at a stream that I could see coming for half a mile through the trees because of the brush along it—and yellow monkey flower growing across it on a fallen log and willow and upstart cotton woods among these dry pine lands. Alongside my horse we pushed our two noses through the cold surface and drank.

It seemed that the water had replaced food, and I thought I might become airy and fey and simply melt into the land. I sat under a tree slathered in the smell of the day and thought I should as a practical matter set my horse free, unburden him of bridle and saddle and send him on his way. My clothes felt like the horse's tack.

I thought that it was this, this emptying out, that I had come halfway around the world for. This is what all the young Germans were really looking for, the sloughing off of the old skin.

I think I was two days, maybe more, there at the center of my losing track of the brewery, a hundred employees, my daughters and wife and business connections. I don't remember eating though I must have. I remember drinking from the stream over and over. I did unburden my horse, but he stayed nearby grazing and occasionally coming to me to stare quizzically about our affairs there. I remember thinking there was no story I could tell the village of Lindenbronn that would make them understand this business of losing everything they valued in the name of what?... an afternoon, two afternoons, maybe more, of sinking back into the original world. I had come to what had become impossible in the old places consumed in custom and habit and tradition.

Joshua might have been watching me the whole time. As in the stories he was chewing slowly, eating something that seemed to take forever. When I saw him across the opening in trees, across the stream, across the two days, he stood watching me and then moved off like a shy deer, and he kept grazing. I wanted nothing by this point and so didn't call to him as I might have a week before. All the things I wanted to know from him seemed immaterial: her death, Otto's bad luck, death and sex at Cummings', the conflated stories of many Joshuas across the West, magic and gold and beer and power. None of these occurred to me there. I sat under the same pine, its orange and black trunk like a vertical tiger, the sunlight making Joshua hard to see as he moved and ruminated, staying away on a perimeter of his choosing. I should have hailed him, interrogated him, got his story and run him to ground like any prey.

Thinking back it seemed not that I couldn't, frozen there like some fairy tale spell, that I couldn't pursue him, but that I only wouldn't. And now I think I was not sure what I would get from him, any more than I could get something by interrogating Pan redolent with goat stink.

I returned to Portland in time to meet with Corbett, Failing and Villard—we four Henrys--about transportation and fiscal opportunities in the coming months. Villard would speak to me in his soft Bavarian German and it drove English Corbett mad. But we managed altogether, to do business.

I found out that the two men Mrs. Els held responsible for beating up her girls—they killed her. They were beaten and embarrassed by her, a mere woman, so they killed her. One of them claimed it was the other—the one recently killed in the woods, pierced by a splinter of fir tree as long as a sword that flew from a tree felled on a hillside and then with the eyes of God's justice, sought out the murderer and pierced his neck and stuck there in heavenly retribution. The other man told the story of his murdering friend's end. How surprised he looked with the apricot-colored and fragrant stake through his neck. How he had stood for a long time holding the wood by both ends, unable to speak, while his blood left his body and he fell into the duff. The reason the survivor told the story was to unburden his soul, he said, to stay God's hand from him. And to tell the world that his partner got what he deserved for killing the woman in Portland.

That was his story, and it came to me by way of Dr. Cruickshank, who had it from one of the lumber camp doctors. The man left the woods to work in the "fields of the Lord," he said, to bring glory to God on earth—and maybe not incidentally, I read into the story, to save himself both on earth and in heaven.

Now I favor the fireplace though my home has central heating—coal-fired and state of the art, the same as wealthy Europeans use to heat their ancestral homes. My wife complains that my fires draw all the steady steam-heat right up the chimney and create drafts in the room. I have kept an old wing-backed chair, the first piece of furniture I bought as a bachelor, though now my wife has reupholstered it several times, not out of wear but to match some carpet or sofa in the room. At the present my chair is wicker and plain, but the blanket is very expensive my wife says. I insist we keep this chair here because it has become essential to my reading and writing, my seeing again all the pen strokes of my story in America. I have a blanket over my knees. I trust my memory more when I see it on the page as if the act of writing also verifies the truth of the enterprise. As with beer, I insist on truth first and foremost. The rest then will come with time.